after breathless

after breathless

Jennifer Potter

BLOOMSBURY

The line 'Poussière, tout n'est que poussière is from the poem 'La Crosse en l'air' by Jacques Prévert, from the collection Paroles (© Editions Gallimard, 1949).

Permission to quote the poem 'Je te l'ai dit' by Paul Eluard, translated by Gilbert Bowen, published by Calder Publications, London, courtesy of The Calder Educational Trust, London.

The song lines quoted are from 'Le Chien' by Léo Ferré, from the album Amour anarchie (1970, Barclay).

First published 1995

Copyright © 1995 by Jennifer Potter

The moral right of the author has been asserted
Bloomsbury Publishing PLC,
2 Soho Square, London W1V 6HB

A CIP catalogue record for this book is available from the British Library

ISBN 0 7475 22480

Typeset by Hewer Text Composition Services, Edinburgh
Printed in Great Britain by Clays Ltd, St Ives plc

FOR CATHERINE

With grateful thanks to
Maureen Freely,
Sarah Tresfort and
Richard Williams

J'aime beaucoup la France.
Si vous n'aimez pas la mer . . .
Si vous n'aimez pas la montagne . . .
Si vous n'aimez pas la ville . . .
Allez vous faire foutre.

– Jean-Luc Godard, *Breathless*

ONE

I never meant to tell this story. Even now, twenty years
after the event, I feel a cringe of shame. Mad love they
call it, *amour fou*, except mad became bad and that's when
our troubles began.

I'm not the sort to be always looking over my shoulder.
'What's done is done,' my mum used to say with a shrug
to her voice and a look like the washing of hands. But
sometimes you can't help yourself. Sometimes the past
slips through the crack and gives you the devil of a chase.
He looked just the same, that's what I couldn't bear, funny
and wise, definitely *louche*. He always looked old to me.

If only Kate had phoned a few minutes earlier. If only
I had switched off the television, gone into the kitchen,
upstairs, anywhere, he would have floated unseen in the
airwaves, out into the fields. 'What's wrong?' asked Kate
anxiously when I finally came to the phone.

'Nothing,' I said firmly. 'Nothing at all.'

'Stephen OK?'

'He's fine. Same as ever. Why do you ask? This has
nothing to do with him.'

'You're really not telling?'

I laughed, or tried to, and said there was little to
tell.

★   ★   ★

1

The two men stand side by side before the open doors of an ambulance. The one holding the microphone hunches under a greasy mackintosh. The other is short. He wears a smartish blazer with a crest on the pocket, its shoulders stained a darker shade of blue by the rain that continues to fall.

The shorter one looks vaguely familiar. You think you might have seen him before, at the cinema. No one really well known. The type who plays sidekick to Alain Delon. Weasel eyes and hair that hangs in rats' tails from the falling rain. Then he looks straight to camera. Not *him*. It can't be. You start counting on your fingers. Thirty-five plus twenty, he'd be fifty-five now, fifty-six at most. The commentator asks him a question: 'How bad is it really?' Something like that. They look towards the ambulance. He speaks broken English: 'May bee okkay. May bee not okkay.' All Frenchmen sound the same. Anyway, you can't see properly. He keeps looking over his shoulder, into the ambulance. Bodies on stretchers. One moves, you think. He turns to face the pack. No mistake, this time. It has to be him, Georges Delvaux, the man you have tried so hard to forget.

You know you shouldn't look but you can't help yourself. He leans forward to shut the door, turns round, raises his hand to camera. His face hardens when you catch his eye, as if he knows you're there. Impossible. Men crowd round the ambulance door. The camera tries to shoot between their jostling heads as the ambulance pulls slowly away. Heads fill the screen. A different camera pans across the race track through billows of black smoke towards a grassy knoll by some trees. You can just make out an upturned car surrounded by milling gendarmes; and a driver, helmetless, who wanders about in a daze.

Defiantly, you switch off the set as the telephone starts to ring, aware of a sudden emptiness inside, an ache in the hole where your heart should be.

Don't get me wrong. It's not the past I wish to re-write now. There are certain things I wish I hadn't done, that's all.

Piranha fish breed in the mind. If you can't see them, they're not there, don't you know? But I can see them, hundreds of them, suspended immobile in the slimy waters of the tank. I'm standing on the rim, looking down. Nothing moves in the tank, not the barest twitch of a tail. A tankful of stuffed fish, that's what you think. And just when you see the sunlight on the water, just when you think you're home free, snap go a thousand jaws and all hell breaks loose. Memories, memories. Ooooooh . . . Worse than dreams.

The rusty gates to the château: they leave a trace of reddish dust in my hands.

No one comes here any more. A notice tacked to the gatepost declares that this is private land, PROPRIÉTÉ PRIVÉE, and underneath – in hand-painted letters – CHIEN MÉCHANT. Georges makes a joke about that. I remember staring at the notice, running my hand across its weathered board. Forgive us our trespasses as we forgive those that trespass against us. My laugh must have startled him. He calls from the car, 'Ça va, toi?'

I say it's nothing really, some childish memory.

The gates creak as they swing open. I understand perfectly that what we are doing is wrong and that my future defence – I am merely a spectator at the wrongdoing of others – is as counterfeit as the promises I have made and will continue to make until the day I leave. My heart begins

3

to race. As I get in the car, Georges slides his hand between my bare legs which are baked brown from the cornfield sun at La Colombe. I hold his head in my hands as he works skilfully at my clothes.

First he runs his palm across the lower part of my belly, kneading it gently so that I feel the heat gathering between my legs. Soon he will move his hand upwards in a smooth sweep, the better to slip his fingers beneath the elastic of my knickers which he will do with a sudden predatory gesture while his mouth sucks at my throat, always the same point beneath the chin. He knows from experience the effect will be instantaneous. Press me here to feel my legs open wide, to feel the arch in my back that helps him ease his body into the right position. We have done this enough times to eliminate all possible snags. I feel the muscles of my mouth go slack.

'No time,' I say brusquely, pushing him off and leaving us both suspended in the warm stew between the salting of desire and its accomplishment.

Georges rests his head against my neck. His breathing comes hard. I wonder if he accepts the truth of my statement: there really is no time.

'*Tu veux pas?*' he says. I think: don't answer, he knows you better than this.

We always wanted each other, right until the end. Even when the love we professed had turned rotten at the heart, even then I wanted him as much as I had at the beginning. Georges felt the same. He said it hadn't happened to him before: to ache for the feel of another's skin, another's sex (he called it my *chatte*, my *praline*, words that made me think of a large fluffy cat stuck between my legs or of Georges, head down, sucking at a pink sugar-coated almond, a dribble of spit on his chin) and to feel, each

4

time, the marvel of surprise. I had so little experience I didn't appreciate how rare it was.

He wanted me, he said, because we were two parts to the same whole. Someone (*le bon Dieu*, I suppose) had split us apart in another life and when we found each other again we slotted exactly into the joints of each other's bodies, each other's hearts. He made a clicking noise with his tongue. 'Shut up,' I said, 'you sound like a carpenter.' From the hurt in his smile I knew he hadn't read Prévert's poem, the one in which the night-watchman pays a visit to the Pope, making me feel superior but sad, too, at allusions we couldn't share.

My reasons – and there were several – were more complicated. Danger featured in all of them. I wanted him because he was bad. Because my family could never approve. Because his past life cast him beyond reach of the law. Because we had sex wherever and whenever we felt like it, in his car, in the fields, in the back streets of Bordeaux. Because he was different, I suppose, and made me feel a stranger to myself. That can be comforting, you know.

We sit side by side. Georges straightens his clothes and leans over to button my shirt. I tell him it's easier if I do it, he'll only want to try again, and so, sighing to himself (but really at me) he re-starts the engine and we drive slowly down the winding track that will take us to the château hidden among the trees.

Tyres swish gently on damp earth. Trees filter the light to a murky green. Fish-tank light. A resinous smell of rain refreshes my senses after the crackling heat of the plains.

I watch him as he drives, watch his face darken as he contemplates our impending encounter with the old lady of the house, the chatelaine of Les Sablons, and I find myself thinking: where will I be in ten, twenty years' time? Who will follow after Georges, the man to whom I am already promised?

Whatever happens, wherever I go, I swear to myself that I shall acknowledge the part Georges has played in my re-invention, Karina to his Belmondo, Jeanne Duval to another's Baudelaire, Dante's Beatrice (except I don't speak Italian). I see my future as a succession of ever more exotic men, painters, writers, poets, alchemists of one sort or another for whom I shall act as their *muse inspiratrice* until the day I find the man I really want to marry. Then I shall settle down, preferably in a large farmhouse where I shall rediscover the simple life at La Colombe, producing the brood of children Georges wants to have with me and remaining grateful to the man who has made my future possible. I might even write to him at times. I'd like him to know how it goes.

We reach the final turn. The château is not as I imagined. A sprawl of turreted shapes and later additions detract from its former grandeur. The place has a derelict air.

Georges stops the car. We sit in silence, reluctant to step outside.

He rests his hand on the leather seat behind my shoulders. 'You seem so far away. What are you thinking?'

'Nothing much,' I say softly, immediately, trying to keep the note of triumph from my voice. I want to touch him but don't. '*Des bêtises* – you know how it goes. Thoughts that lead nowhere.'

Towards a future I never had.

TWO

I blame it all on Arthur Rimbaud, Jean-Nicolas-Arthur Rimbaud to give him his full name, poet, iconoclast and gun-runner who sparked what little sense I have of revolt. *A la lisière de la forêt*, at the edge of the forest, the words come tumbling back and with them a glimmer of that breathless intensity, a blend of enchantment and *ennui*, of high drama and silliness interspersed with long periods when nothing much occurred. God, how bored I was most of the time, so bored I could scream if anyone mentioned God again, or the absence of God, or whether a chair is really a chair if you aren't there to observe its chairness. It's years and years since I've held one of those conversations, but then . . .

I was one of the moon-faced girls in the University French Department. We formed a threesome: myself, the Francophile Rachel Plante who married a painter and went to live in Montmartre, my best friend Kate whom strangers often mistook for my twin. We looked alike, I suppose: tallish, dark-haired and somewhat forbidding though we laughed a lot, among ourselves. People judged me attractive then: not pretty, not stunning either – I have this pastrycook's nose and terrible feet – but good enough to make it to Rag Queen candidate. For the Engineers, I should add. Didn't win. Didn't make it to the first eleven but came a respectable twelfth which pretty well sums me up.

For the contest I was dressed in see-through chiffon that barely covered my bum and forced to perform a skit with hairy-chested engineers masquerading as cavemen. The microphones didn't work properly so no one caught a word we said but the drift was plain enough. It was my first lesson in the humiliations incumbent on those who court a certain popularity.

In fact, despite my several boyfriends and the sleight-of-hand required to keep them apart I was rather lonely underneath. Friday nights saw me at the local supermarket buying a bottle of beer, always the same: light-brown ale.

'Washing your hair again, dearie?' the cashier would say with a smirk.

I never explained that the bottle was really for me. I would drink it back home in Alma Road Avenue stretched on the window seat of my second-floor room while I waited for the doorbell to ring and when it did (always late) I would stand behind the curtain looking down to check if it was John instead of Edward, or the other way round, or maybe someone else, and if they all arrived together I'd pretend I wasn't there.

Mostly I went where they wanted, to the union bar and on to an obligatory party where loud music took the place of conversation and cheap wine soured the spirits then back to the flats they shared with their friends for a desultory hump in the dark. They acted like boys, adopting a variety of funny voices because love-talk didn't come naturally. And they never changed the sheets. I could only hope that the widening circle of whitish stains was evidence of my previous visits and not those of other girls whose books and belongings I sometimes found abandoned near the bed. I felt too uncertain of my rights to ask.

Early in my second year a new boyfriend took over my

life: Henry Marchfeld, French and Drama, distinguished by meatloaf thighs and an unpleasantly loud theatrical laugh. My initial resistance was soon overcome and it was understood, at least by me, that we would marry when we had finished the course. God knows why. I didn't even like him much and that laugh got right up my nose. Several years later he went blind after a car accident but after a string of operations eventually recovered his sight. I was glad about that.

Henry dumped me unceremoniously for a voluptuous Polish girl with enormous boobs (we called them that then) and a Mini-Cooper car. It wasn't fair: I could offer only a rickety bicycle and a very flat chest. For a time I was devastated, flunked my term's exams (which thankfully didn't count) and thought of taking a year's sabbatical to 'sort myself out'.

My friends pulled me through. Rachel dismissed him out of hand. One look at the sketch I had made of him in the Berkeley Café – the only sketch, I should add, which is surely significant – was enough to convince her I was off my head. 'What's that?' she asked, pointing between his legs.

'Umm, well, it's a . . .'

'Looks suspiciously like a codpiece to me. Henry VIII, you know. He's even got Tudor legs. Can't you see it?'

'I suppose he does a *bit*. But he's not like that at all.'

'Don't you believe it. Hung like a horse and fickle as hell. They're all the same, honestly.'

Kate joined forces with Rachel. 'What on earth do you see in him?' she asked repeatedly, as if her baby-faced dentist were anything out of the ordinary.

'He flattered me, I suppose. The way he sort of takes control. He's *very* insistent.'

'Flattened more like. He's built like a tank.'

'And he made me feel different. I don't know. Like he calls me Jan when everyone calls me Janey.'

Rachel laughed like a hooter. 'Big deal.'

'Suit yourself,' I replied huffily, though I knew they were right. He really was a jerk.

I was over the worst of my heart-break when the three of us left for Bordeaux in March 1969: *Cours de langue et de civilisation françaises*, the usual thing. The majority of students lived in town – Prusilla something, engaged to a probation officer in Leeds; Bev and Daphne and clever Mr Jones, we all called him that. I passed three years of my life in their company and remember little about any of them. Henry Marchfeld went to Avignon with the rest of the drama crowd.

Kate and I lived at Talence-Pessac within walking distance of the university campus, sharing a wooden summer-house at the bottom of the Gilberts' garden, an elderly couple related by marriage to one of our course professors. We also shared a double bed, stuffing a bolster down the centre to keep us apart. No men. That was the principal rule. Otherwise we were free to come and go as we pleased.

I found the place dull. Bordeaux was hardly a hot-bed of *soixante-huitards*; the revolution had passed us by. *Métro, boulot, dodo* with the occasional distraction of a party in town – what a way to spend your youth when life was taking shape elsewhere. Rachel had stayed long enough to register then disappeared to Paris to join her boyfriend, a painter she had met the previous year when forced to share his café-table at the Louvre. She wrote to say that life with André was like living through a perpetual seminar. Despite her terrifying choice of simile I found myself consumed with envy for her artist's garret in Montmartre while I grew steadily more sullen in our double bed at the bottom of the Gilberts' garden.

The morning of the day I met Georges dawned cold but bright. It was late March and our first taste of spring. Kate made coffee, as usual. She hadn't screwed the coffee-pot together properly so when the water boiled a few drops hissed in a streak down the side. We sat bare-armed on the step. One of us (undoubtedly me) had forgotten to put away the milk in the small fridge the night before. Seeing the creamy-white globs float to the surface of Kate's cup, I chose to drink my coffee black. It tasted no worse than the cut-price espressos I bought (and rarely drank) from the student canteen. It was anyway suitably *authentic*, a word I had only recently started to use.

After a time I went inside to change. Purple lambswool sweater, blue-checked miniskirt that hugged my figure well, soft leather boots in a very impractical pale cream.

Leaving Kate sunbathing on the steps, I set off for class. Monsieur Gilbert hailed me from the top of his step ladder, secateurs in hand. '*Bonne journée*,' he called, with a rakish lilt to his voice. I felt his eyes on my legs as I banged the gate behind me.

I didn't hear the car at first. My head rang with the gravelly tones of Léo Ferré, anti-hero of the Left Bank whose latest album I had recently bought: *Amour anarchie*, songs of love and revolt and under-age sex *pour épater la bourgeoisie* enlivened with dirty words that invariably sound better in French.

11

'. . . *et si vraiment Dieu existait| comme le disait Bakounine| ce camarade vitamine| il faudrait s'en débarrasser|* . . .'

The hooting of a car horn made me jump into the roadway. Behind me I saw a flashy white car, an Opel, I think, with headlights that swivelled up and down like the eyes of a toad. Seizing on my dazed expression, the driver wound down the window, intending to make some *ho-là-là* remark. That made me stew. (It still would if anyone gave me the chance.) I moved closer, intending to make a suitable riposte, *tu me casses les couilles*, something like that, when I recognised the passenger, a spotty medical student I had met at a student disco arranged to make us feel 'at home'.

Without a clear plan I walked towards the car, its passenger now plainly as embarrassed as I was.

'*Ça va, toi?*' I shook his hand awkwardly through the open window.

'*Ah, oui,*' he replied, flustered. '*Et vous? Comment allez-vous?*'

I had been too familiar as usual. I said I was well then added, because no one knew what to say, that I found the city dull. '*Pas grand'chose, vous comprenez.*'

The driver took this as a personal affront. 'We are holding a party tonight,' he said peremptorily. 'A *surprise-partie*. You must come. Then you will discover we are sacred monsters underneath.' He bared his gums for my benefit.

'Where is it?' I asked the spotty one. He shrugged. The party had taken him by surprise, too.

His companion wrote an address on a scrap of paper. Waving it at me through the window, he caught hold of my hand. 'You will come, won't you? I count on your company.' He pressed his damp lips to the underside of my wrist.

'Perhaps,' I said, retrieving my hand and wiping it up

12

and down my skirt. 'That depends.' Depended on what I wasn't sure. The man was clearly a creep.

But I went all the same, taking Kate with me for company. She needed a night out as much as I did. It took us ages to find the right place. By mistake I left the street plan in the bus and as we couldn't afford a taxi, we were feeling out of sorts by the time we finally arrived.

The driver of the flashy white car opened the door himself. Slim hips and a continental cut to his trousers. His name was Daniel.

'So you have come at last,' he smirked. 'I knew you would. And you have brought a friend, how nice. Charming, in fact.' He reached for Kate's hand. She pushed right past him and entered the darkened room. Rolling Stones on the turntable. Several couples danced with varying degrees of enthusiasm. No monsters, I'm afraid.

Before I had time to make my own escape Daniel marched me over to the drinks where he poured me cheap red wine in a plastic beaker (I'd been here before, many times) then stood unpleasantly close, jigging his pelvis in time to the beat. To make himself heard above the juke-box tunes and sparky conversations he had to speak directly into my ear, nauseating me with whiffs of over-spiced cologne. I thought grimly of Henry Marchfeld.

'You like Frenchmen,' he said. 'I see it in your eyes, beautiful eyes, my dear, has anyone told you that? Of course, we understand you women so well. We know your little ways. As for the English . . .' He let his scorn trail off into a Gallic shrug.

It was very crude. 'You call yourself a man?' I said rashly, letting my eyes rest on those sleek hips that stopped jigging suddenly. Through his tight trousers you could see his (medium-sized) balls. 'I don't think

13

you know *me* at all. The English, yes, they have their faults. They can be boorish at times, uncultivated, if you like, there are exceptions, but my dear friend, *mon cher*, *ils sont quand même des* hommes.'

Daniel turned his back on me, buttocks protruding like neat grapefruits through the fabric of his stretch pants. I was so angry I wanted to hit him. Or leave. I looked round for Kate. She was already entwined on the dance floor with a lanky French youth who looked more or less OK. After all our efforts at finding the place it didn't seem fair to drag her away so I poured myself another beaker of wine and joined a group as far away from Daniel as possible. He seemed equally anxious to keep his distance from me.

There was only one person in the room who looked remotely interesting. A fair bit older than the others, he sat by himself on a heap of cushions in one corner, a lighted cigarette permanently dangled from his lips, arms clasped loosely around a battered guitar which he would beat now and then like a drum. It was his face I liked best, the way it displayed the knocks and bumps of experience like a second-hand car, an old Mercedes or an Alfa-Romeo, something fast and foreign with the tawdry glamour of the track. I am perhaps reading too much into first impressions but it seemed as if his manner carried a secret invitation though he never looked at me once and I never tried to respond. There was nothing I could say, no one had told me his name, and I felt obscurely that to talk with him would break his spell.

As the evening dragged boisterously on I found that whenever I glanced towards this tousled figure in the corner my stomach went soft inside.

The numbers started to dwindle.

It was Daniel who announced the party had died. To liven

14

things up he proposed a drive to the coast. He would take one group in the Opel, the others would go with Georges. I didn't care who this Georges was as long as I stayed clear of Daniel.

Kate wanted to leave. I said we should stay for a time. Who knows, we might even enjoy ourselves.

The party split into two. Kate, poor soul, was claimed by Daniel. I went with Georges.

It was he, of course, my man with the soundless guitar.

Suddenly shy, I climbed into the back of his Renault Gordini. We touched accidentally as he opened the door. My heart turned over as I stared at my feet. He mumbled something I couldn't catch.

Throughout the riotous drive to the coast the girl in the front seat, the seat next to Georges, talked non-stop. She sounded madly sophisticated, evoking, I noticed, little response from Georges. Pressed between two others on the back seat I watched his hands on the wheel, admiring the strength in his arms, and though we drove alarmingly fast with Daniel stuck to our tail, I wasn't afraid. I wanted our drive through the night to continue for a long, long time.

At Arcachon we turned off the sea-front, pulling up outside a low block of flats. The first lights of morning had entered the sky: it must have been around 4 a.m. Daniel rang one of the bells. I asked what he thought he was doing.

'My cousin lives here,' he said coldly, 'Paul and his wife Martine. *Pas mal*, you'll see.'

They took for ever to answer the door. I can't say I blame them. Nor did they seem too pleased at the prospect of playing host to the surly remnants of a *surprise-partie* that had fallen flat.

Paul and Martine, both naked, returned to bed. Paul had

the scrawny body of a young Boy Scout while his wife was built like a Titian. Even I could see their funny side. Georges had stayed behind in the car.

'Help yourself to food,' said Daniel, waving his arms towards the kitchen.

Kate went to the bathroom. She came back quickly and hissed in my ear, 'Have you brought any Tampax?'

I shook my head. 'We could always ask her,' I said, pointing to the busty blonde in bed. 'What do you call them, anyway?'

'Tampax, I expect,' said Kate tartly, which made us both laugh. Daniel became quite nasty when I refused to share the joke. Things were plainly getting out of hand.

When the others had finished raiding the kitchen cupboards, we trooped outside.

Georges was leaning against his car, staring at the sky. His car was shiny blue. French racing blue, I later discovered. That mattered, to him.

As we walked past the car he fell in step with me. The others went to the beach – we could hear them larking about – while Georges and I continued alone to the end of a small wooden jetty overlooking the lagoon. The sun was just rising from behind the sea.

We stood for a time in silence. He was about my height, a little shorter, if I'm honest. The sea clopped against the jetty in the soft dawn light.

'*C'est beau*,' I ventured at last. I mean, I had to say something.

He gave me a quizzical look and then, without a word, kissed me gently on the forehead, a kiss like a bird's that hinted at passion to come.

I felt his lips on my skin. Saw our future rise majestically from the waters of the lagoon like the hazy pink sun, shimmering among the clouds. I know it sounds soupy but that's how it felt, I promise you. The world hung upside down. *Les fleurs de rêve tintent, éclatent, éclairent.* Arthur Rimbaud again. I told you he was largely to blame. The freshness of the breaking day caught in my throat.

'You're shivering,' he said. 'Here, take this.'

There was a moment's awkwardness as he wrapped his jersey around my shoulders. Its oiled wool smelt of the sea and the dusty road. His hand on my neck generated a series of rapid electric shocks. I felt my skin peel open until my nerve-ends screamed for him to stop. (Touch me there, please, there, there, don't listen when I beg you to stop.) I longed to bury my hands in the crinkly surface of his face, explore from within the cracks that radiated from his eyes. He was old. I didn't care. He would teach me things I couldn't even dream.

We stood and stared at each other. My smile felt glazed. My whole life felt glazed and I wished I could do something that would make me worthy of his attention.

The illusion of time stopped still was broken by a chorus of shouts from the beach. I tried not to hear. We had swapped our ordinary selves for vaudeville conceits. This princess loves a frog. Ah yes, but frogs become kings, inherit the kingdom that is rightly theirs.

They shouted again, Daniel's voice rising above the rest.

He shrugged. We were standing so close I could see myself in his eyes. I knew he wanted me as much as I wanted him, I could feel him pressed against my skirt. He should have brought his guitar: I would have danced for him then on those rickety boards, followed him blindly into the dunes, done anything he asked of me (the things we later did) but because he was older than I and very much

17

the wiser, he knew that we should take our time. Neither fools nor angels, I suppose.

'We should go,' he said, his voice low and vibrant. 'They're calling to us. It's very late.'

'*Vraiment?*' I felt his arm about my neck.

'No, it's early. Maybe five in the morning. We must go home to sleep.'

'I can't ask you in.'

'I know. I mean something different, you'll see. I don't even know your name.'

'It's Janey, Janey Wilcox.'

'*Génie?*'

'*He is affection and the present, puisqu'il a fait la maison ouverte à l'hiver . . . à l'hiver . . .* Sorry, I can't remember the rest . . .'

'You don't say.'

'Rimbaud, my favourite poet. A poem called "*Génie*". You know him?'

'Not personally.'

He turned towards the end of the jetty. I felt suddenly fretful. Perhaps he didn't like poetry. Through the gaps in the boards the sea looked sandy brown, flecked with eddies of foam.

Together, we walked unsteadily to the beach where Georges lifted me down, his hands slipping easily round my waist as he lifted me into the air. He seemed to like me. Sand filled my shoes. I walked on air after that, holding my shoes in one hand, Georges in the other. The smile on my face had begun to feel like lockjaw.

They were waiting for us by the car, Daniel with his backside pressed against the Opel's window.

18

'*Tiens,*' he sneered when he saw Georges holding my hand. '*Elle fait la noce, la nana.*'

I scowled back at him, uncertain what he meant. Then I saw Kate beckoning to me from the other side of the car and went over to join her. In a furious whisper she said that while they had been fooling about on the beach Daniel had grabbed her from behind and tried to pull her into the dunes. He'd bloody nearly raped her. If she ever set eyes on him again, she would eat his balls for breakfast. I promised to lend her a hand, suggesting she should come back with us.

This time she sat in front at Georges's insistence. He knew she was my friend. The talkative girl was bundled into the other car. I sat, as before, in the back, only this time instead of staring at the set of his shoulders, at his hands on the wheel, I kept my eyes on the mirror, to be rewarded by sly smiles of complicity whenever we slowed for the lights.

Kate and I were dropped off first.

We neither kissed nor exchanged addresses. He knew where to find me.

The curtains in the main house twitched as we tiptoed up the garden path. Madame Gilbert, disturbed by the slamming of doors, was peering down at us from the landing window. Her face looked grimly disapproving. She shut the curtains the moment I waved. I didn't care. As the sound of his car disappeared into the early morning I felt the world vibrate with such sweetness I wanted to shout my joy to the whole neighbourhood. They could go hang themselves, the Gilberts and all the others who sought to disapprove.

I was young and had fallen in love for the first time. I wasn't to know – how could I? – that I might never get the chance again.

THREE

Insistent knocking broke through my dreams and a truculent male voice, a cross between a peasant's and a Spanish waiter. '*Vous êtes là, Mesdemoiselles?*' My eyes felt glued together with pieces of grit.

'*Ouvrez la porte, s'il vous plaît.*'

Footsteps clattered down a dark wooden hall. An old man wearing an enormous black beret flapped his arms at the far end. Monsieur Gilbert, our landlord.

'*Ouvrez. Ouvrez.*'

I sat up in bed and looked at my watch. 10.35 a.m. You couldn't mistake that voice but what the hell did he want?

Kate, fully dressed, was peering through the blinds of the bedroom window. 'Here,' she said, throwing me a pair of old jeans. I must have looked pretty vacant.

'Put them on,' she insisted, 'now.'

I stumbled out of bed and hopped into the jeans, stuffing the tails of my frilly nightdress into the belt, then followed her into the kitchen.

The door opened before I was ready and Monsieur Gilbert poked his shiny potato head into the room. He had never appeared without his beret before and wasn't as bald as I had assumed. His head had a covering of goose down, so soft you wanted to stroke it against the grain.

Without crossing the threshold he peered left and right, his look of expectancy dissolving into disappointment when he saw my class books open on the table where I'd left them the previous night. His eye continued along the wall, pausing momentarily to examine several sketches of Georges stuck on with Sellotape (against the rules surely?) then down to a stack of empty wine bottles beside the bin. At this he made a loud popping sound with his cheeks.

'Come outside, if you please,' he said stiffly. 'I want to talk with you.'

I made sure that Kate went first. The air was cold and I felt the bumps rising up the bare flesh of my arms.

He looked first at Kate then at me. 'You have no classes this morning?' he asked.

We both shook our heads. Only Kate was able to meet his eye.

'That is not good,' he said. '*C'est pas bong, ça*. You must work hard. Not everyone is clever enough to go to *university*. I shall tell my son-in-law they do not work you hard enough these days. I was saying to Madame only this morning, those girls have too much time on their hands.'

'We work non-stop,' I protested. 'Kate always comes top.'

'That's good. Very good indeed.' He beamed his approval at her. I felt myself beginning to prickle. 'However. I come to say something else. I have told you before but . . .' He shrugged. *Bof* said his face, no one listens to me. 'You know the rules of this house. No men here. *Pas d'ongs ici*.' I thought he was saying sorry. Sorry for what? Kate nodded swiftly.

'Not even I,' he went on. 'I am a man, after all, am I not?' He stared at my frilly neckline, an icy twinkle to his eyes which dropped to the bulges in my jeans.

21

Absent-mindedly producing his beret from a back pocket he stepped into the flowerbeds to get a better look at us. Cluck, cluck went his tongue, a puzzled shake of his wily old head. 'You two are very different, *vous savez*. Cluck, cluck, cluck. If I wanted *une maîtresse* . . .' He took my hand, giving it an unpleasantly sharp squeeze. '*Pas de choix, vraimang*. You'd suit me very well . . . As for you, *mon enfang* . . .' He bowed towards Kate, without touching her (that was significant, I felt), 'I would choose you *pour ma femme*.'

Kate blushed. I wanted to slam the door in his face. But by then I was already sleeping with Georges and had no right to complain.

It happened in his car which we had parked on the edge of a hill overlooking the city. Hazy mist hid the spires of Bordeaux. The day felt very warm. We could have sought shelter in the grass. It was a regular beauty spot: anyone might have seen. But instead we closed all the windows which quickly steamed up. I suppose it didn't take long. The gear stick got in the way. The seats reclined only so far, no further. You had to be very athletic to make proper contact. *Génie, Génie*. Georges's face close to mine, his stubble scraping against my cheek as he called out my name. I remember the suction of black-leather seats and the insane jangle provoked by his touch.

Afterwards we opened the doors and sat staring at the view. My legs were open on the seat. Anyone might pass – so what? For the first time in my life I wasn't embarrassed by the act of sex, nor did I feel awkward. If people didn't like what they saw that was their problem, not mine. Georges placed a lazy arm behind my neck, rubbing his hand against my ear while attempting to fasten his trousers with the other.

'Both hands,' I said, 'you need both hands. Let me do it.'

I couldn't work the zip. '*C'est un mystère*,' I said.

'What has happened to us?'

'No. Your clothes, stupid. Maybe I am just too tired. I feel I'd like to sleep for a hundred years.'

'Dangerous. One day you will wake up like Reep Van Winkle and find the world has changed.'

'You know the story too?'

'Of course. He was American, I think. Not English, anyway.'

'I suppose not. Jack the Ripper, he was English. You should have seen what he did to his victims. Turned me vegetarian for months.'

'He sleeps too, this man?'

'No more than anyone else.'

Georges looked baffled.

'Rip, reep, ripping – when you said it, it made me think . . . oh, never mind.'

'You tell an English joke?'

'No, that's just it. I wasn't trying to be funny.'

The fact that he had misunderstood gave me a strange sense of power. My foreignness allowed me to behave differently from the Janey I knew.

'Let's go home,' I said suddenly, 'to your place. I really do want to sleep and we can't go back to Kate's. The Gilberts would sling me out.'

'I don't think that is possible,' he said carefully. My head was buried close to his chest. I felt his voice vibrate in my hair.

'Why not? You never take me home. I want to see where you live, where you sleep.'

He looked away from me, wiping the window with his hand.

'Because, my little *Génie*, I don't think Madame Delvaux would approve.'

It took several seconds for his statement to click into place. When it did, I sat up straight, catching my head on his chin with a loud snap.

'What do you mean, Madame Delvaux wouldn't approve?'

'There are certain *convenances*. We must respect the rules.'

He was laughing at me now. I felt angry and confused. He was married. Of course. Why the hell hadn't I thought of that before? He didn't act like a married man. He seemed too wayward for that, too free. You can tell when men are cheating on their wives. That's part of their game. But Georges was different. He didn't seem to be cheating on anyone.

'You could have told me,' I said, unable to disguise the hurt in my voice. 'Take me home. Now.'

'Back to Kate's?' he asked, taunting me with his smile.

'Yes, back to Kate's. Wherever. I don't give a damn where we go. You could have told me this before. It's possible I might still have . . . I don't know, Georges. But to tell me like this, after we've . . . after we've . . .'

'After we've what, my little one?'

'I'm bigger than you are.'

He laughed at this, laughed out loud. His behaviour was intolerable, grinning like a monkey that had just poked its genitals through the cage. He looked like a monkey too. I would have chucked a whole bag of nuts at his face. He reached out to switch on the engine. Thinking he meant to touch me, I slapped him hard.

He stopped smiling. 'You should know me better than this, Janey.'

'I thought I did. But I was wrong, wasn't I?'

'Oh Janey. Madame Delvaux is my mother.'

'Your *mother*?'

'She wouldn't approve at all. You see, she's very correct. I can't simply arrive on the doorstep and announce that we're going to bed.'

'You live with your mother? But, Georges, that's crazy. How old are you?'

'Thirty-five. I didn't always live at home. I was married once. I have a child too, a little boy. His name is Pascal.'

'You have a son? How old?'

Georges counted on his fingers. 'Seven or eight. I don't see him any more.'

'That's terrible. Does your wife . . . past-wife . . . forbid you to see him, or what?'

He didn't reply. The sudden noise of the engine broke the stillness of that warm afternoon. Reversing at speed we passed a couple of hikers on the track. They side-stepped the car, looking annoyed at our intrusion. One of the men shook his fist. I wished they had seen us before, seen Georges squatting between my open knees. This was our place now: they had no right to come.

'Can't we stay? I mean, maybe we could go for a walk, if you don't want to . . .'

'Haven't time. I'm working tonight.'

'Not even here in the car? It wouldn't take long.'

He stopped the car and caught hold of my wrist. 'You have a taste for it, I see.' A memory flashed past, uninvited. I pushed it away.

'With you, yes. This is different, Georges. You must understand that.'

'How different?'

Why do they always want to know? I thought of that

other man, a businessman from Düsseldorf who had driven me one dark and stormy night to a wood on the outskirts of the city. I let him kiss me on the back seat of his fancy-flash Mercedes. Silly fool. A struggle ensued between my pantihose and his awakened lust. The pantihose won.

'Just different.'

'For me it is the same.' He let go of my wrist. Still confused, I wanted him then with a sharpness that took me by surprise. It had never been like this before. Cross my heart and hope to die, that's what lovers do.

'And I shall tell you something else. I knew as soon as I saw you what would happen between us.'

'On the jetty, at Arcachon?'

'Before that, at the party. You were talking with Daniel, your eyes shining like beacons.'

'I was angry with him, that's why.'

'Then lose your temper with me, *mon ange*.'

His words stroked me like a caress.

He looked me straight in the eye. 'If I marry again – when I marry again . . . You know what I'm saying, don't you?'

I nodded dumbly.

'Then we needn't speak of it now. Later, one day soon. *Je t'aime*: I think you know that, *ma chérie*, and for the moment that is all that counts.'

How can you tell when someone speaks the truth? I was only nineteen. If I don't know the answer now, what chance had I then? And anyway, I'm not sure the truth mattered. It wasn't for me a question of belief but rather of make-believe. 'Loving' was as easy as philosophy. I think therefore I am. I feel pleasure therefore I love. I hurt therefore I am loved. I am, I am.

★   ★   ★

26

The first time I found him parked in the street outside the Gilberts' house, almost a week after the night of the *surprise-partie*, I had given up hope of ever seeing him again.

Kate noticed him first. 'Isn't that whatsisname?' she asked with a nudge and a nod towards the blue Gordini. I passed her my books, said goodbye and ran towards the car. If the curtains twitched, I didn't bother to look.

Georges started the engine then almost as an after-thought, kissed me lightly on both cheeks.

'Where to?' he asked.

'Anywhere you want.'

'You choose.'

'We could go to the ocean, if you like.'

And so we did, roaring down those long straight roads with just a kink by the poplars. You didn't wear seat belts, in those days. I doubt if they were even fitted. Seat belts were chicken, anyhow. We went to Lacanau, not yet open for the season, where we ate *steak frites* at formica tables overlooking the sea-front. The steaks were chewy and grey, ribbed with charcoal burns – horsemeat, probably. He asked me to choose a song from the juke-box selection at our table. Flicking through the plastic wallets, I chose his namesake, Georges Moustaki. *Avec ta gueule de métèque, de der de der de dededer, de voleur et de vagabond* . . . The song became a theme tune for us, played in beach-side cafés.

After we had finished our meal we walked along the front to the dunes. Doorways banged in the wind. The place had a Wild West feel to it. We talked about this and that in the way strangers do, skirting the quicksands of our emotions.

In the dunes, Georges produced his cigarettes. I produced

mine. He smoked Rothmans. I smoked Gitanes. We made a joke about it, part of our cultural cross-dressing, then lay in the cold sand, watching clouds scudding in from the sea. We must have held hands and once he climbed on top of me, though nothing serious took place.

'I like your friend Kate,' he said, turning on to his stomach and digging his elbows into the sand.

'Everyone does. She's very popular.'

'Daniel doesn't.'

'Daniel? The man's a prick. I don't expect he cares for me, either.'

Georges laughed. He looked very impish, at times. 'I think you have him wrong, Janey, he likes you very much. Only, he told me, between ourselves, that you and Kate are, you know.'

'I don't know. I haven't a clue what you're talking about.'

'That you and Kate, well . . .' He looked away from me, back towards the sea. 'That you sleep together here in Bordeaux.'

'Who on earth told him that?'

'Kate herself, apparently. At Arcachon. They had some dispute. Kate told him she'd rather sleep in her bed with you than with a . . . something not very polite . . . like him.'

I snorted.

'So it's not true?'

'No. I mean, yes it is. We do share a bed together. But we put a . . . what do you call those things, a pillow like a long sausage down the middle. Kate must have wanted him off her back. She can't abide fools.'

'A long sausage?' I nodded. He grinned. I wanted him to hold me in his arms. 'Oh Janey, that's OK,' he said, moving closer so that I felt his breath on my neck. 'I don't want to share you with anyone.'

When I got home, late that night, I didn't tell Kate about this conversation. From now there were many things I would keep to myself. Curled against the bolster, listening to the even sounds of her breathing, I wished she were someone else.

I had often imagined the things that men might do to me, the things I would do in return, but in a way that was curiously chaste. The men always had their faces blanked out, their limbs the consistency of suet. Only their penises were hard, as hard as Henry Marchfeld's blundering about my body as he turned our love-making into a performance in which I took a very subordinate role.

Georges had felt as light as the bolster under which I slipped my right leg, feeling its lumps with my thighs pressed close. Kate turned over in her sleep. Strands of her dark hair spread about the pillow. I saw her mouth open in the half-darkness, saw the covers rise as she breathed, up down, up down, wishing it were Georges watching me and that he might wake me by placing his hand down there, feel its sticky invitation, there, there, that's right, you know what I want, don't you, you know *exactly* what I want and the longer you play catch-as-catch-can in the dunes the wetter, stickier, it will become.

Georges was the clever one. I see it clearly now, the way he gauged the precise measure of my gullibility and my equal hunger for Romance. He fed me morsels himself, coaxing them down my eager throat, a hint here, an allusion there to events that cast a shadow over his life and served merely to increase his attraction. The first hints he dropped

29

in the dunes: a judge had called him, in open court, the scum of the earth. That's all I knew. I imagined it had something to do with a woman, his wife, I would later conclude, though at the time he hadn't mentioned her existence, and that he had somehow driven her to kill herself. For love, *bien sûr*.

When he repeated the judge's words, I nearly cried. It seemed a monstrous thing to say. 'I want to help you,' I said with the solemn foolishness of my nineteen years. *Je veux t'aider*. Georges misheard my reply. Our life together was built on these simple misunderstandings. And when I finally discovered the truth about the judge's words, from someone else, it was too late to make an inkling of a difference. '*Je veux t'aimer*,' that's what Georges thought I said.

FOUR

Like, love, lust: who knows when one slips into the other, when liking shades into lust or when love becomes so hopelessly entangled your only recourse is to cut yourself free? The question worried me more than it did Georges who had no time for semantic hair-splitting; *enculer les mouches*, he called it, buggering flies.

Words tie you up in knots, that's what Georges used to say, distrusting my ability to slip from one language to another in exactly the same way he distrusted my facility to catch his likeness with a few flicks of my pen. He didn't much care for the results: said I made him look too old, too short, too this, too that, an object of ridicule – tenderness, actually. Mum reckoned I was good enough for art school. Dad said no, use what brains you possess.

I was always sketching that summer: in the margins of my notes, on napkins from cheap cafés, sometimes on squared paper bought specially from the university stationer's. There was only one sketch Georges liked well enough to keep: a cartoon portrait of him at the wheel of his Renault Gordini, his expression infinitely world-weary like Jean-Paul Belmondo in *Breathless*. Sacred Monsters, I called it, *Monstres sacrés*, words dashed in red ink across the top of the page. I liked it best, too, of all the drawings I did.

31

I gave it to him by the ocean. We stuck it to the windscreen of his car and then made love, our only audience the gulls who had seen it all before, the car down below parked away from the others, a woman's (girl's) shameless abandon as her lover wrenches at her clothes, *non, non, vraiment*, hands clawing at his neck, the cry he makes when the tide bursts and she feels the warm, pulsing trickle between her legs but she isn't ready to stop, he's gone too fast, and so she must squeeze her thighs round his hips, pressing the heel of both palms into the small of his back until she, too, climbs higher and higher until at last she lets go and swoops over the edge; and after a breathy silence, the man's delighted whoops because he swears the face in the sketch winked at him over her shoulder as she finally lay still.

When it was all finished between us, I took my remaining sketches home to England and made a bonfire of them in the garden, torching each one individually and watching the curl of flame seep across the page like a dark brown tide. Mum caught me tipping the ashes into the rose beds. It was one of those late September days, glowing ripe and yellow, the sort of day that makes you glad to be alive. We shared a joke about it, pretending I had scattered the ashes from a dead man's urn. She must have known what I had done.

However childish it seems now, the bonfire cheered me up by allowing me to say sorry for my unspeakable behaviour – not to Georges, of course, whom I had left behind, but sorry to myself. I wish I hadn't done it, though. I wish I had kept at least one of the sketches of Georges as a reminder of how he looked then (or how I saw him) so that I might understand whether what we felt was love or some more physiological compulsion, an itch in the pants triggered by the discrepancy in our ages (my fresh-faced youth, the taint of his age) and my own *nostalgie de la boue*.

Last night I was feeling so low, I called Kate. She was putting the boys to bed and couldn't talk for long. I asked her straight out whether she remembered Georges and the times we had together in Bordeaux. 'Good heavens,' was her immediate reply, 'what on earth made you think of *him*?'

I knew I had made a mistake in mentioning his name but she wouldn't let go and I couldn't help but be impressed by just how much she did remember. For a time we had gone round together in a foursome, myself, Georges, Kate and Georges's friend Bertrand (bit of a goon, she called him). They worked together in an out-of-town supermarket on the road to Périgueux. 'Was it Suma?' 'No, Carrefour.'

'He didn't mean to stay there long,' I went on quickly, 'he wanted to go to Le Mans, become a racing driver.'

'Well, yes,' she replied dubiously, 'we all have dreams. Hey, remember the time Monsieur Gilbert found the two of you in bed together, in the summer-house? Old thingummy was so livid he looked as if he might drop dead. *La rage*, you know, mad dogs and Englishmen.'

'But Georges was French,' I protested.

'Of course he was French. That was the point, wasn't it? Georges was different. You said the same about all of them.'

She went quiet all of a sudden. I should have let the conversation drop, asked her about the boys or her husband Peter who works in a merchant bank, something big in foreign aid, but I had to know what she was thinking.

She didn't want to say. Either she was afraid she

might offend me or she really wasn't sure what the matter was.

'There were times,' she said carefully, 'when he frightened me. When I didn't know if he was good or bad.'

'You sound like the boys, like Sam,' I said, trying to turn it into a joke.

'You must have seen it yourself. There was something very hard beneath the clowning and the games. You said he was mixed up in things. I haven't a clue what they were. You became very secretive. I didn't mind. Not much, anyway. But I worried for you sometimes when you didn't come home. And after you'd left the Gilberts' the police came looking for you. Something about a book, a dictionary. You'd warned me, so it wasn't too much of a shock, but you should have seen the old boy's face when he brought them up the path to the summer-house. Did anything happen? Anything terrible, I mean. Perhaps I shouldn't ask. It's all so long ago.'

I felt a sharp pain below my diaphragm, like the turn of a rusty screw. Had I forgotten that too?

'No, nothing happened,' I said quietly, more to myself than to her, 'nothing happened at all.'

After we have said a cool goodbye, I think: there was a photograph. What happened to that? It was certainly spared the flames. I remember pinning it to the wall beneath my favourite Magritte poster (the man who looks in a mirror at the back of his head) and I didn't buy that until *after* the ritual burning.

I found it eventually, the photograph of Georges Delvaux, stuck down the side of my grandfather's metal deed box. It's where I keep the few things that matter: Stephen's wedding ring, the one I never wore; a letter from the clinic telling

34

me the worst; cryptic postcards from Kate; old passports; letters, letters, letters (none from Georges and a bare handful from Stephen); a sepia photograph of my mother as a young girl. I had searched here first without success and only looked a second time because I had tried everywhere else.

As I shut the lid, I noticed a corner sticking out near the hinges. That's why I hadn't found it before. Count to ten, slowly now, don't want to rush, then release it from the metal rim.

The photograph is small, about two inches by two and a half, matt black on the underside, the word 'Polaroid' and a number stamped at the bottom. Both edges are serrated, as if it has been torn from a strip.

The camera puzzles me. I have never owned a Polaroid and don't remember photographs like these. A small pinhole at the top suggests it has indeed been pinned to a wall.

I turn it over in my hands.

His face leaps out at me from the box, the mouth contorted with half-suppressed laughter, laughter in the dark, recalling all the mad, indecent things we did together. Stephen is fine, better than fine, he's one of the best, but we don't exactly have a ball. I look again. He's wearing the same jersey he lent me on the jetty at Arcachon, navy blue with buttons across one shoulder. The photograph is black-and-white. I still remember the smell. The photograph starts at his chest, outlined against a background of chalky hills on the other side of the valley. Which valley is that? It seems unreasonably important.

His smile in the photograph. It reminds me suddenly of Rimbaud. The opening lines to a poem called '*Mauvais sang*', Bad Blood. *From my Gaulish ancestors I inherit my blue*

white eyes, narrow brains and clumsiness in strife. My clothes
strike me as barbarous as theirs but I don't butter my hair.

That's *it*, that's him exactly, you think with a dozy grin,
remembering how you had read him the lines as you lay
together in the dunes and how he had grabbed you round
the waist saying he was far too old, too ugly to be confused
with the drug-crazed ramblings of some *pédé* who drove
people mad enough to shoot him. Well, Verlaine had a bash,
didn't he? And anyway, he could think of better places to
poke his nose than a stuffy old book. Throwing Rimbaud
over a hillock he pushed you down into the tufty grass of the
dunes, into its seaweedy smell, his hands tugging at your
underwear as you tried to ward him off, responding to his
shouts with cries of your own and after a time you don't
fight any more, your head full of clouds, remembering how
it felt when you climbed on top of him, saw the sand in his
hair, shifting position to the point where it hurt – not what
you intended but you won't complain.

His smile has turned a little crazed, bug-eyed, as he
thumps you up and down, holding your buttocks with his
hands, surprisingly large hands with thick stubby fingers
that tighten their grip until you are moving in exactly the
way he wants, the way you want too, flat out like greased
pistons that turn the cogs, that turn the wheels, that make
your knees shift in unison and you don't even stop when
two startled heads appear over the dunes, a woman and
a little boy, the woman shielding the boy's eyes with her
hands, *Viens vite, chéri.* You see the whites of his eyes, hear
the noise he makes with his teeth, amazing, like grinding
corn, one last gasp as his head rolls backwards, wait for
me, can't you please wait for me.

You press your own fingers there between your legs and
roll over on to the pillow, forgetting that Stephen might

have crept up the stairs, that he might be waiting outside the open door, watching your reflection in the mirror that invites you to step through the glass into the wind-swept dunes where you climax as noisily as he had done and you lie side by side listening to the ocean, unseen, and the low hooping of gulls, returning to the summer-house long after sundown with tell-tale scratches on your sunburnt knees and a bucketful of sand in your knickers which you empty surreptitiously over Monsieur Gilbert's tomatoes.

FIVE

K ate was right: there was a dangerous side to Georges Delvaux though not, I think, in quite the way she meant. To call him crooked is to miss the point: his moral ambivalence was simply a habit, an attitude borrowed like his fast cars from an uncle, the bent *garagiste*, and he shared most things (myself apart) with an openness of spirit that made others look mean. It's what attracted me to him: his past was marked on his forehead as surely as Cain's. My childhood transgressions were much the same as any other's: trivial theft, trespass, sneaking on the boys next door, nothing grand or even serious. I was too easily scared for that. But Georges's sins (whatever they were) had landed him in court and whole parts of his life were kept deliberately shut away. That time in the café, for instance, when Georges's refusal to explain his encounter with the man I later knew as Jean, Jean *le grand* and other names besides, left me with a lingering unease.

It was a place we often frequented: a workman's canteen near the docks where you sat at long trestle tables bunched in with dockers and blue-overalled mechanics, their faces camouflaged with grease, paying for wine by the centimetre which the *patronne* measured with tape. After the first few times no one paid me the slightest attention beyond a casual glance at my legs.

The door was open to the street, admitting the fumes and dust of a hot spring day. Steep steps led down into the room. Lorries thundered past towards the port, their wheels at eye-level. Georges and I didn't talk much. Nobody did. It wasn't that sort of place.

Without waiting for our order, the *patronne* brought us platefuls of lamb stew. I wanted something light. She said she'd bring me a salad, later, but only if I cleared my plate. At first I had mistaken her sharpness for a Frenchwoman's customary dislike of foreigners and liked her more when I realised her manner was the same with everyone.

I had just started to eat when a shadow fell across my plate. A man stood framed against the sunlight, arms crossed, a real wardrobe-type. I couldn't see his face.

The man nodded at Georges. Georges looked at me. What was I supposed to do? Without a word of explanation, he pushed back his chair and went to the door. I know Georges was small but his head barely reached the other's chest. I saw the *patronne* shake her head with annoyance as if she didn't want the giant inside.

After exchanging a few words, Georges gestured to me that he had to go out. Pointing at his watch, he held up the fingers of one hand. Five minutes. We'd see about that. Light filled the room. The men had disappeared.

I ate as slowly as I could. Five minutes rolled into six, into ten, into twenty. The lamb was tender as a bird. By the time the *patronne* brought me a huge bowl of salad I was no longer hungry. I spilt some wine on my shirt and had to brave the WC downstairs. A man was urinating in the unlit cabin, its door partly ajar. Someone else had apparently declined to wait and used the basin instead. In the airless corridor, the stench of urine and other people's faeces made me retch. Breathing through my mouth, I stabbed at the purple stain on my shirt, turning my back to the cabin door when I heard the cistern gush.

It was a relief to return to the heavy smells of *ragoût* and haricot beans upstairs boosted with occasional bursts of diesel fumes. The *patronne* had cleared away my plate, leaving a dish of melting ice-cream. I asked for coffee but the espresso machine had broken down. I didn't want tea.

After a full thirty minutes I got up to pay. By now the café was virtually empty and I had seen the last two youths whispering together in a corner and casting sly glances in my direction. At the till, Madame refused to let me pay for Georges. He would settle his own account, the next time he came. She tapped at my sleeve as if she wanted to tell me something but the youths came up behind, uncomfortably close, so I took my change and left.

Outside I stepped without looking into the roadway, narrowly missing collision with a speeding bicycle. The man swore over his shoulder as he wobbled past. Shaken, I looked left and right and started to cross just as the blue Gordini roared through the lights at red. Georges braked hard when he saw me. I jumped for the pavement and hurried on up the street, followed by Georges hooting furiously from the car. People stepped aside to let me pass. They could see I was mad about something.

At the crossroads, I heard the car door slamming.

'Hey, Janey,' he said, tugging at my sleeve, 'what's the hurry?'

I stopped suddenly. He banged into my back. 'You said you wouldn't be long.'

'OK. It took longer than I thought. You don't have to storm off like that just because I say ten and stay away twenty.'

'Thirty. No, nearly forty, now. And you said you'd only be five.'

'Five, ten, thirty. I can count too, you know.'

'That's not fair.'

'Fair, fair. Don't come to me if you want things to be fair. I'm fed up with it. *J'en ai marre*, Janey. Fed up to here.' He drew a line across his throat. 'If you want a fight, pick someone else, someone more your size.'

Without another word, he went back to the car he had abandoned on the kerbside. Sound of door slamming a second time.

I hesitated. He sat behind the wheel, staring straight ahead. There were things I should do at home: books to read and essays to write. My professor, Monsieur Gilbert's son-in-law, had already called me in for a 'little chat'. While I had never been a model student, they had at least expected me to try. At the end of the interview he handed back my hasty essay on Rimbaud, remarking that its stream-of-consciousness effects were positively Joycean. 'But you were asked to produce an essay, Miss Wilcox, not *Ulysses*. Unless we see some improvement, a formal warning is the best you can expect.'

Go home, said a voice. Play it safe. Safe as houses. I don't want a house. I want to be free. Georges means more to me than all the rest. More than Rimbaud? No, but that's the whole point, don't you see? Not at all. He makes you angry. Hot and angry as hell. If I weren't angry, I wouldn't feel me. It's like that chair all over again. If you can't see it, you can't be sure it exists. So Georges isn't real? I looked towards the car. He was sitting bolt upright, eyes front. Selfish bastard. They're all the same: expecting you to wait while they run around God knows where. I won't be gone long. Fuck you.

Georges swivelled his eyes. He was looking at me now, pretending not to see but he saw me right enough, I could tell from the smugness of his smile. Better go home. Nothing for you here, unless you want to spend the next God knows how many years waiting for that rat-face.

Hey, come on. What's half an hour between friends? So he said he'd be back sooner. Big deal. Why get mad just because he made you wait?

As I watched, undecided, he leaned over and opened the car door on the pavement side, catching a woman who trailed two small children along the kerb. She shouted at him angrily. *Cretin. What's happened to your eyes?* He shouted back. I laughed, I'm afraid. He called her a fish stew. She dragged the children away, still shouting abuse over her shoulder. Georges raised his hands in mock despair.

I got in the car. He leant across to shut the door.

'I tried to pay for you,' I said, 'in the café. Madame wouldn't let me. She said she'd get the money from you, next time you went. You won't forget, will you?'

'Listen, Janey. Let's get things straight between us. I don't need you to tell me what I will or won't do. That old bitch (he called her a mackerel) will get her money when it suits me.'

'OK. OK. Now take me home, please. I've got things to do. Work, essays, you know.'

He pulled a mincing face. I nearly got out again. 'This is stupid,' I said. 'Who was he anyway, the one who came to the café?'

'A friend.'

'Some friend. What did he want with you?'

'That, my little Janey, is none of your business. Don't ask and I won't lie.'

I couldn't tell what he was thinking. We were both angry

42

with the other, each convinced we had the better cause. He took me home, squealing the tyres on purpose. We barely exchanged a word. At the Gilberts' he kissed me on the mouth but only because Madame Gilbert was watching from an upper window, then drove off without arranging to meet.

I tried unsuccessfully to work. When my essay petered out (heroes and anti-heroes, this time) I went to the campus in search of Kate, whom I found working with the others in the library. We sat on the grass outside. I told her what had happened in the café and even did for her a drawing of the mysterious gorilla who had come looking for Georges. She said he reminded her of her Uncle Percy, which made me laugh.

When Georges turned up in the street after a week's agonised silence, I was suitably contrite and vowed to myself I wouldn't nag him again nor would I ask about the 'friend' who had called for him at the café. I found out soon enough.

Big Jean. I still owe him money, three hundred francs. Blood money, you might say. His family name remains a mystery. Men like that don't have names – not ones you can trust. Georges was fast teaching me the rules of this shadow world to which he held the key. Rule number one: keep your mouth shut. Rule number two: keep your eyes open but don't let anyone see. Rule number three: keep your nose clean and if you have to use a handkerchief, borrow the next man's. Rule number four: when you hear the whistle, run like hell.

SIX

It wasn't always like that. Most of the time we simply had fun, propelled by Georges's capacity to spin his life in a perpetual present tense unshaded by grammatical subjunctives, by the futures, pasts and future conditionals that bothered me.

He called me his doe, his dove, his *julie*, his *cocotte*, his little cabbage (this last to make me laugh, one in the eye for Henry Marchfeld). My face was like a flower, he said, soft and petally; my *sexe* an open wound. Come closer, I replied, and feel me bleed. We said these things and we weren't embarrassed at how silly we might sound to anyone else. As for my hips, my *ligne de hanches*, he said they'd look perfect in a grass skirt, absolutely magnificent, dancing to a Polynesian guitar. I wiggled them like he said, without the grass skirt – without anything on at all.

There were parties, outings, pranks, car rallies (once was enough, for Kate), another nocturnal excursion to Arcachon with many of the original crowd (not Daniel, thank God, who had gone away). Georges played his guitar on the beach under a deep black sky. As his *petite amie* I lay in the sand at his feet, warmed by the certain satisfaction that his words were meant only for me. There was also the cinema. Screenings at the university and sometimes in town. Languid afternoons holding hands in the dark.

44

Blatant necking in the middle row, his hand up my skirt. *Pssst. Mais c'est incroyable. Qu'est-ce qu'ils foutent là-bas?*

'In the crossways of kisses, the years pass too fast.' Jean-Luc Godard. *Breathless*. Those were our words spoken on screen, our lives underscored with a soundtrack that accentuated the leaps and bounds of our affair, the hidden menace as they tightened the screws. 'Informers inform, assassins assassinate, lovers love . . .' Yes, that was it exactly, that was Georges and I in glorious black-and-white.

The ending took me by surprise. *'Qu'est-ce que c'est dégueulasse?'* 'As I'm treating you badly, it proves I'm not in love with you.' 'When we talked, I talked about me, you talked about you. It's more complicated than that.'

Afterwards I cried. Georges, patient as a lamb, dabbed at my tear-streaked face with a dirty handkerchief and asked what was wrong.

'She betrayed him. That's terrible.'

'It's only a film.'

'You don't understand. They shouldn't have let it happen. Not the girl, she did what she was told, but Godard. Why do you men arrange things so that they come out best?'

Georges shrugged. 'It happens,' he said, non-committally.

Not to people like us.

Some time in June Georges drove me to Paris to visit Rachel. Classes must have stopped for a time or maybe I just bunked off. That part has become vague. I remember the geography professor chalking the names of French towns on the blackboard, the capitals of various departments, including those of *outre mer*. Otherwise my life in the classroom has vanished into a black hole. I thought of asking Kate to come with us – Georges was keen – but she had recently stopped seeing his friend Bertrand and two seemed a safer bet than three. I bought her several bottles of decent wine as a peace-offering, to drink while we went away.

We took the fast road through Angoulême and Tours where Georges suggested a detour via Le Mans but didn't object when I said I'd rather go by Chartres instead. Here we headed straight for the cathedral, a vast sombre cavern crowded with stiff-necked visitors and bored family groups. In the candle-lit gloom Georges's face took on the dubious piety of an altar boy. *Angells affect us oft and worship'd bee* . . . I hadn't read any Donne at the time so why do I think of it now? *But since my soule, whose child love is| Takes limmes of flesh, and else could nothing doe* . . . If there were anything else, Georges and I hadn't discovered it. We held hands like children in the night, scuttling past worried priests to admire the great rose windows, the Gothic conquest of mass and space.

Beside the statue of Our Lady of the Pillar he halted. The Virgin looked Chinese. So did Her Son. A bank of votive candles cast a sheen on Georges's face.

A candle for your thoughts. Hush, don't tell. Jesus only likes you if you sin. As Georges reached for the box, I felt the rising of a shrill scream. You *hypocrite*. He couldn't possibly believe such trickery.

A glance at his sober face told me he could.

His coin clanged into the box.

It's for her, isn't it, this flaming candle of yours? Your wife, I don't even know her name, the one who killed herself, or was that someone else? Someone who loved you too. Your wife, her, your little boy, where is he now? Don't, Georges. Don't do it. Please. Look at me. If you light that candle, I shall scream. I shan't be able to help myself.

It's growing louder every second. They're all staring at me now. Pressing round about. Someone touched me then. I felt a clutching at my sleeve. Everyone hears but you.

Clamping both hands to my ears I shut my eyes tight. Georges stepped back. He must have lit the blessed candle, I didn't see, but when I opened my eyes again the flames flickered and pulsed in tiered rows, so many promises soon to be reneged. This was for her, not me. I didn't know which was his. I took a gulp of air and blew as hard as I could, hard enough to extinguish at least half the candles in the rack.

Then as an Angell, face and wings| Of aire, not pure as it, yet pure doth weare . . . I turned and fled, scattering a posse of nuns. My shoes clattered on the flagstones. Startled glances and feet that got in the way. Schoolchildren clamoured around the exit. I cut a path through the middle and ran through the doors, eager to escape the sickly incense smell. Out on the steps the air felt fresh. I bent forwards and touched my toes. Blood flowed back to my head.

Georges found me sitting by the south door, flanked by demons and the damned. The demons had cloven hooves and pixie ears. One had a naked woman slung upside-down on his back, a human head embedded in his belly. Lips that leered where men had other things. Horrible.

'*Mon Dieu*, little *Génie*, what's wrong?' I shook my head without looking up, forcing him to kneel beside me on the steps where he gently cupped both hands about my chin. 'What happened back there? You caused quite an uproar.'

I refused to answer. A priest had appeared through the doors, face as black as the cassock that swirled about his sandalled feet. He hesitated when he saw my face. Men are useless with tears, even priests.

47

'I'll make it up to you,' said Georges, sitting beside me on the step.

'How can you? You don't know what's wrong.'

'I know you better than you think.'

'Better than I know myself. It was her, wasn't it,' I said angrily, 'the one you were praying for back there?'

'Who? Our Lady of the Pillar?'

'Her, you know, the one who . . . Shit, you know who I mean.'

My voice continued to rise. The priest was joined by a second. They were obviously talking about me. I looked away. Some poor devil was being shovelled into the mouth of Leviathan. Better that than the pallid pleasures of Abraham's bosom on the far portal.

'Anyway,' I scoffed, 'prayers like that never come true, take my word for it. If you think the world will change just because you light a candle in front of an effigy . . .'

His hand sketched a face in the dust. My face, I think. It had an outsize tear trickling down one cheek.

'I'm sorry you say that,' he said, sadly or mockingly, I couldn't tell. 'I hoped that this one might work. I prayed for us, you see.'

We ran away from the cathedral feeling ten feet tall. Georges held my hand. Jazz-café sounds and a beat that made me want to shout. I matched him stride for stride. We had the devil in our shoes, Georges and I, and it was only when we had left the town behind that I reminded him we hadn't eaten all day and he had promised to buy me a sandwich. We were still laughing when we pulled into an Alpine *auberge* in the forests around Rambouillet where they gave us a room under the eaves, a room with narrow windows that opened to the floor, a view across trees towards a reedy lake.

As they were already serving dinner we ate straight away: a slow meal, partly to savour what came next and partly because the young waitress was drunk and kept forgetting our orders. She had probably been out with the cook. Everything was off except vegetable soup, over-done pork chops and Chantilly ice-cream. We stayed for brandies after the few other diners had gone, most of whom complained loudly when they saw the size of their bill. Georges left the waitress a large tip because he liked her, he said, not because he felt sorry for her.

Arm in arm we climbed the steep stairs to our room, Georges with an unfinished bottle of wine concealed under his shirt. It was the first time we had shared a real bed together. I couldn't help giggling at his underpants. Droopy and white, they matched his little boy's vest. He responded by laughing at mine, which weren't funny at all.

The bed seemed enormous, its mattress soft as down, or so it seemed to us after the squeaky harshness of the car's leather seats. The luxury of sheets and a room to ourselves: we made full use of it that night, making love crossways, lengthways, sometimes on the floor and once kneeling by the open window where trees glowed green in the moonlight. Our exuberance kept others awake. People in the next-door room banged on the wall and someone threw pebbles from the drive. Georges responded by shouting – naked – from the balcony. Then he leaped into bed and we laughed like idiots until I stuffed a pillow over my head and nearly choked.

When at last we turned away from each other I fell asleep straight away.

The next morning I opened my eyes to find Georges sitting up in bed dressed in vest and pants, maps strewn across the

49

sheets. He claimed to have taken a walk already to watch the mist rising off the lake but I don't think he had: his trousers lay heaped with mine, his shoes by the door where he had kicked them off the night before. We talked about whether we would go by Choisy or Versailles, made love, missed breakfast and cleared the room just before noon.

The red-eyed waitress brought us coffee while we waited to pay the bill. As he put his wallet away, I saw that Georges had little money left.

SEVEN

On the outskirts of Paris, I telephoned Rachel from a café. My letter hadn't arrived so she wasn't expecting us. I found her invitation to visit a little offhand.

It was late afternoon before we finally located her apartment off the rue Gabrielle, having abandoned the car in the twisting streets of the Butte after we had driven a third time past the awning of the *Lapin Agile* and Georges said they obviously didn't teach map-reading at my university. Rachel answered straight away, impatient at our lengthy delay. She was looking very French in trousers and a plaid shirt, her smoky brown hair cut in page-boy style. As she led us upstairs she said they had friends coming to supper. We could eat with them too, if we liked. I wasn't sure if she meant us to accept but Georges said fine, he'd like that very much. We hadn't eaten well the previous night. He related the antics of the waitress and succeeded in making her smile.

André was waiting to receive us in the brown-painted living room (nigger brown, we called it then), the four walls hung with examples of his art. He wasn't at all as I had imagined him. Artists, I thought, were instantly recognisable, larger-than-life dishevelled creatures who communicate their intensity in sharp bursts like the shock you get from sticking your fingers up a socket. André was

51

tall and dark, yes, but plump as a pampered cat. Shaking his hand was the feline equivalent of being stroked by a wet fish. In this case, however, the man was infinitely preferable to the work.

The centre-piece of his *oeuvre* was a sub-Cubist portrait of Rachel, nude, floating across a backdrop of sludgy tones that ranged from a murky undersea green to a particularly offensive dog-shit brown. Rachel herself was bright baby pink. Various parts of her deconstructed anatomy had been slung together any old how: ballooning breasts, a jewelled hand emerging from a point below her ears, skinny thighs, feet splayed like flippers and the portrait's focal point placed conveniently at eye-level: a gaping maw of peeled-back pudenda clamped around a used bus ticket stuck upside-down.

I didn't know where to look.

Georges had no such inhibitions. Stepping closer, he shifted his eyes from the portrait to Rachel and back to the portrait, transfixed by that blasted ticket which I thought for an awful moment he was going to peel away. How on earth could she live with it, day in, day out? That's what I wanted to know. And what artistic licence had allowed him to inflate her breasts to these beach balls? Her chest was almost as flat as mine.

'*Incroyable*,' muttered Georges.

'It pleases you, I hope,' said André.

'Very much.' Georges's face had turned pink like hers.

André looked expectantly at me. I coughed. When he came too close he smelt like a barber. 'Yes. Very nice. Very nice indeed.' *Joli* was the word I used which in retrospect seems hardly appropriate. 'What's it called?'

'*Aller et Retour*,' he said impatiently. 'The bus ticket. If you look closely, you'll see it's printed down the side.'

Choosing to take him at his word, I glanced warily at the others. One or two I rather liked, especially a haunting water-colour of Rachel's face peering out from beneath a large straw hat. The rest were shit.

Rachel took me into the kitchen. I was dying to ask what she thought of them herself and what 'sitting' for André entailed. Did they talk while he painted? Did they sometimes take a break? I mean, what do artists *do*, faced with such an invitation of naked flesh and only the pretence of a paintbrush to keep rogue hands properly in check. What would any man do? She didn't oblige, launching instead into a long tale of André this and André that but not the things I wanted to know.

According to Rachel, he would soon join the first rank of his contemporaries. Already he was quite well known. A small, highly select gallery on the Ile St-Louis had asked to see his latest portfolio. A bookshop in the *quartier* had offered to stage an exhibition. *Le Canard Enchaîné* had recently devoted a whole page to his cartoons.

'So he does those too?' I tried to sound impressed.

'They're not what you think,' she snapped. 'The French take their cartoons seriously.'

I wondered what I had done to offend her.

Eventually she ran out of things to say. 'How are things with you two?' she asked as she busied herself over the stove.

'We're fine. Georges . . .'

'I meant you and Kate.'

'Kate's well. She sends her love. Actually, she's a bit fed up. Bordeaux's pretty ghastly and she hasn't found anyone yet. There was a friend of Georges's for a time; he was OK but that didn't last. The ocean is the only good thing, we go there quite a lot, weekends, after class sometimes. Why don't you come and see us?'

'André says we'll get married next year, after I've passed my exams.'

'That's great. I didn't think artists did. Get married, I mean. You must be very pleased. André's . . . great.'

I was on the point of telling her that Georges and I had similar plans when André called from the other room, asking her to make coffee. Obligingly she put the pot on the stove, waited until the hissing and bubbling had stopped, then asked if I would take the tray through to them as she must get busy with supper.

'I thought you'd waited in for us. If there's anything you need to do outside . . .'

'Too late now.'

The men were busy talking as I manoeuvred the tray through the door. That was odd. I wouldn't have thought Georges was André's type.

'I cared for it once,' André was saying, 'when you could tell there was a human being at the wheel.'

Georges looked annoyed. 'What do you mean?'

'When you could still see their faces. Now – they're so cosseted with safety gear they might as well be dummies inside.'

'You think that's wrong?'

I said, 'Here's the coffee.'

André grunted then looked earnestly at Georges: 'It didn't bother Fangio much, did it? He went out with his polo shirt, his cork helmet and his slip-on shoes and just got on with it. He came through all right.'

'I think if you did it yourself, you'd see the point of a decent crash helmet. And a flameproof suit.'

'That's just it. You're brave enough to want to do it, I'm not. You can provide all the safeguards in the world, all the flameproof gear and the crash barriers, but drivers will still get killed. That's why people go to watch. Not me but the others. They want to see somebody crash. Don't you think about it when you drive?'

'Me? Oh you know, as Janey will tell you, I'm far too busy to think about crashing. Anyway,' he looked at me and laughed, 'I'm immortal.'

Rachel, bursting in on us from the kitchen, clearly thought he was off his head. When he saw her, André started to inspect his fingernails. They were very clean.

'If you want to see the *quartier*,' she said, looking pointedly at Georges, 'you should go now. Yves and Hélène are expected at seven-thirty. You don't want to be late.'

Annoyed at this obvious dismissal I followed Georges downstairs. Rachel had said that when we returned she would throw us the key from the kitchen window. I said we could take the key with us to save her the bother but she said no, they had only the one key and this was how they did things. She asked us to buy wine, and butter from the *épicerie* as they hadn't enough for six.

We bought the wine straight away – four bottles of red. Georges had to borrow money from me: I suggested two was surely enough but he said my friends didn't look like drinkers and if we were going to stay the night we should lay in stocks.

'She hasn't asked us to stay, you know.'

'She will. And if she doesn't, we'll go to a hotel. You'd like that, I think. How about Pigalle?'

'We don't have any money.'

'That's easily found. Why else should I bring you here?'

55

He kissed me among the wine bins beneath the assistant's casual stare. I was feeling hungover from the night before. Brandy doesn't agree with me. I wondered why I always forgot.

We walked a long way, trusting to Georges's sense of direction. Triangles of brilliant sunlight illuminated the upper storeys, tilting the street to a false perspective. Cars blocked the pavements, forcing us into the roadway. Several times I clanked the bottles against their bumpers.

This is Paris, I thought, the Paris of dreams. A little boy peed into the gutter, spraying my feet as I passed.

Down a steep flight of steps we found ourselves in the African quarter, trailing after men and women dressed in gaudy caftans and tea-towel hats. The buildings and shops looked poorer, the vegetables more exotic. On our return, the steps seemed to go on for ever.

Back in the rue Gabrielle I remembered the butter. It was now dead on seven-thirty. Rachel's *épicerie* was closed but we found another in a side street. Also about to shut, they let us in reluctantly. Rachel had told me exactly where to find the right brand, instructions that were useless here so I bought the one that looked most appealing and we reached their apartment at seven-forty-five.

I suppose they were talking inside and didn't hear my knock. We waited for ages. Georges said, 'To hell with this, let's go home.'

'Home – where?'

'Back to Bordeaux.'

I kissed him and said he was mad.

Eventually the concierge let us in and we had to bang on the door to their apartment. Rachel came to the door, thanked Georges for the wine then looked at me and said,

'I knew you weren't listening. This butter's salted. André won't eat it.'

'It's all I could get. The shop was closed. We had to go somewhere else.' I told her the name of the shop. She said, 'We never go there.'

The others stopped talking when we entered the room. I took to Yves at once: he had an intelligent face, fine-boned with hair that fell in a mare's lock over his forehead. He was a writer, Rachel explained. I shook his hand and liked the way he smiled at me. Hélène was minute, immaculately turned out in a pierrot suit of red and blue checks with contrasting bobbles on her shoes. She made me feel instantly clumsy. It's my feet, I'm afraid. There's nothing I can do about them.

'Hélène's training to be an actress,' said Rachel. 'She's already landed a part in one of the Boul' Mich' theatres.'

'Just a very small part,' said Hélène, smiling angelically through narrow Siamese eyes. 'I've only got one line. One word really: *angoisse*, but I say it all the time. I'm playing a tombstone.'

Yves rescued me from the embarrassing pause that followed by making room for me on the divan. You either slouched or sat bolt upright and after trying both I settled for the floor. Georges, hands behind his back, walked the length of André's paintings, pausing far too long in front of Rachel's portrait, then sat alone on a hard wicker chair beside a pile of magazines. He picked up a copy of *Marie Claire* and started flicking through the pages.

The other four had been discussing a Dali retrospective at one of the galleries. I hadn't seen it, of course, but surrealism was one of my special subjects, I could even beat Kate, and with Yves's encouragement I was able to talk quite entertainingly about the paintings I knew.

I began to see that approaching life as a seminar had its attractions as Rachel and I took turns in discussing the significance of soft clocks, lunacy, bad taste, *trompe-l'oeil*, the slitting of eyeballs, Lautréamont's umbrella, Antonin Artaud's letter to the Dalai Lama and Dali's man with shit-stained underpants.

After a lengthy disagreement about the literary merits of automatic writing – and whether 'merit' had retained its currency as a critical concept – the two women disappeared into the kitchen where I heard them chattering like sparrows. Rachel's French had certainly improved. André returned to his nails. Yves gave me a special smile and said, 'You know Dali took Gala away from Eluard; she became his lifelong muse?'

I shut my eyes.

'*Je te l'ai dit pour les nuages* | I said it to you for the clouds | *Je te l'ai dit pour l'arbre de la mer . . .*'

'You know it too,' he exclaimed, squeezing my hand as a compliment. 'It's one of my favourites.'

'For each wave for the birds in the trees | For the pebbles of sound | *Pour les mains familières . . .*'

We said it together and when we reached the last line I glanced at Georges who had rejected *Marie Claire* in favour of an old copy of *Paris Match*. *Toute caresse toute confiance se survivent*. Yves turned to me with a barely perceptible shrug. 'What do you think of Dali, Monsieur Georges?' he called across the room. 'You haven't yet shared your opinion.'

'The man's a fraud,' said Georges gruffly without bothering to look up.

From then it only got worse.

On Rachel's instructions Yves and André carried the kitchen table into the living room. There wasn't room for six of us by the stove, she explained, placing me next to Yves and directly opposite the bus ticket. Georges was given an upturned box on the opposite side. He made a lot of noise with his soup. Sorrel soup, Rachel said. It tasted suspiciously of soil. I noticed André helped himself to the butter I had bought while Hélène pecked at this and that which was just as well because supper was sparse and Georges had taken far more than his share. We ate several salads, all variations on the theme of tomatoes, followed by the same ingredients served warm as a vegetable stew.

Hélène told us about her play. The lead – Chopin's ghost – was played by an asparagus of an Anguillan wearing a cassock. Apart from herself the cast included a Yugoslav with a crew-cut and a Chinaman who couldn't speak French.

'What's it about?' I asked, struggling to visualise the scene. Hélène helpfully explained that plays didn't have plots any more, just situations.

To prevent any comment from Georges – he seemed to have discovered something very strange about the ceiling – I started talking loudly to Rachel who asked me to speak French in deference to the others. As I was telling her about Kate I didn't think that mattered but André was kind. He said he hoped Kate would pay them a visit when she next passed through.

After we had finished eating – and Georges had drained another bottle of wine – Rachel addressed Georges directly for the first time that evening. She asked him what he did.

'I work at Carrefour,' he said, staring at his plate.

'Carrefour?' She looked puzzled. I think she thought it was a publishing house or something. 'What do you do for them?'

59

'I work on the meat counter,' he replied, glancing at me.

He knew I'd be furious. He was shifted from meat months ago.

'Georges plans to become a racing driver,' I broke in quickly. 'He also plays the guitar. You should hear him – he's very good. Maybe you'll play for us after supper?

'Not without my guitar, I won't.'

'But we brought it with us. I saw it in the boot of the car, last night.'

'The strings are broken. Not possible, I'm afraid.'

Yves said, 'Don't force him to play if he doesn't want to.'

In the silence that followed Georges poured himself more wine, keeping hold of the bottle by his plate. I glared at him across the table. Yves unfortunately got in the way. 'Is something wrong?' he asked. I had to laugh it off and we started talking about Tolkien.

'The English have such a talent for the supernatural,' he said, moving closer so that our elbows touched. 'It's my theory you have the weather to thank for that.'

'The weather's not *that* bad.'

'You don't understand. I think your weather is magnificent. All that endless rain, it drives you inside, turns your thoughts to other worlds.'

'Does it?'

'Can I take it you don't care for Tolkien?'

'To be honest,' I said rashly, 'I never got past the prologue. Big folk, little folk . . . it's a bit fey for my taste. Of course,' I went on quickly, aware of the pit that had just opened up beneath the dinner table, 'lots of my friends like him very much. There's a chap in the English department who regularly holds Hobbit parties. Ask Rachel.'

'I think Tolkien's marvellous,' she said, 'and *such* fun. I was reading him just the other day. He's got terrific imagination. I don't care where his ideas come from, they're jolly good.'

She collected the dirty plates and carried them into the kitchen, Hélène pattering at her heels. I would have gone with them but Rachel shut the kitchen door. I heard them talking on the other side. Hélène was making actressy noises of a man eating soup, a very boorish man. Georges, obviously. Shrieks of laughter from Rachel. Hélène's squeaky voice continued her imitations. She may have started on me. I found it hard to listen properly to Yves who was now stuck on clouds (meteorology was evidently a pet subject), while Georges and André had returned to cars. Their conversation consisted of the names of French racing drivers followed by epithets and insults of varying degrees. '*Il est con, celui-là,*' was Georges's inevitable response to any name proposed by André. 'That one? *Tu parles . . .* Couldn't steer his way out of a paper bag.'

Rachel came back with some tea. I said – in English – that I'd rather have coffee. She said – in French – they didn't drink coffee at this hour. Coffee was a stimulant. We would be awake all night if we drank some now. I said she could drink what she liked but *I* wanted coffee. I'd make it myself if I had to. Determined to ignore me, Rachel sat down and started talking to Yves.

I got mad, I'm afraid. Maybe I was drunk. I said – still in English – that a few sleepless nights never did artists any harm. Rimbaud practically lived on the stuff, and drugs. As a *real* artist, you had to push yourself to the limits. Couldn't sleep . . . Wouldn't sleep . . . Since when had she got so bourgeois in her tastes?

'You weren't that fussy back home,' I went on, aware

61

that I couldn't stop myself now even if I had wanted to; I was hurtling down the slope on my toboggan, Dad hollering and yelling from the top of the field just as Georges was wagging his finger furiously from the other end of the table, *Jump, for Christ's sake, you're heading straight for the wall*, but with the wind blasting my face, the whooshing of hard-packed snow, I knew that it was far too late to think of letting go, I could only hang on to the end, to the moment when I crashed head-first into the stone wall, saw the lights go out in a flashing of stars. Never been the same again, Dad thinks.

Rachel opened her mouth. Saliva glistened on her shiny white teeth.

'With friends like these you don't want to step out of line, is that it?' I said, feeling a swoop as we went over the hump and down. 'I heard what you said in there, you and Hélène, well, not exactly heard every word but enough to know what you meant. You were laughing at us, weren't you, laughing at Georges and me? Perhaps someone could explain what's so bloody marvellous about crouching on your knees pretending to be a tombstone. At least they won't have to prompt. *Angoisse, angoisse*. As for André's paintings . . . Kindergarten stuff if you ask me and I should know. Just because Georges works in a supermarket you think you can sneer at him. He'll make it one day, make it right to the top and then who'll look the fool?'

I heard the noise of furniture falling over. Georges was tugging at my arm. 'I think it's time to go,' he was saying, smiling at the others as he pulled me to my feet. 'Janey's tired. You must excuse us, we really have to go. Thank you. Thank you.' Smiling like a half-wit, a real *minus* that one, left his marbles behind. I tried to shake him off. Yves was kissing me goodbye. Why do all the men here look like cats? Not Georges but the others. Cats' eyes. Cats' piss. Rachel looked furious, sitting like an old *mémé* at the head of the table. No wonder André had added a bus ticket. From his vacant expression I knew he hadn't caught a word. Hélène let off a tinkle of a laugh that started high and carried on rising. I wanted to slap her face but Georges was pulling me out of the room, his hand clenched tightly around my upper arm, into the hall and down the stairs, clatter clatter, out into the street where I finally shook him off and stormed on ahead, walking so fast that I soon got lost, weaving left and right down streets chosen at random, not slackening my pace until I found myself groping down a narrow dark alley that wound back on itself then came to a dead end.

Three sides of tall shuttered houses stretched above my head. A smell of garbage in the air. Feeling trapped, I stopped. For a moment there was total silence. Then I heard Georges's footsteps pelting round the corner. If he hadn't come to my rescue I don't know what I would have done.

'They were laughing at you in the kitchen, couldn't you hear? Rachel and that smug little clown. What a midget.'

'Of course I heard. So what? People like that . . . I don't care about them.'

His cigarette burned red in the alleyway.

'But *I* care, Georges, I care very much. Rachel's my friend.'

'If Rachel is your friend you should have treated her better.'

'So it's my fault, is it? She shouldn't have laughed at you. She must have known we could hear. I think she was making fun of me as well.'

'People do things without thinking. Don't bother about them. It's not worth it.'

'I wanted them to like you, and now . . .'

He threw his cigarette away. 'And now you know they don't. Those arty types, they don't care for grocers.'

His cigarette burned on the pavement. He stamped on it and said that if I wanted his honest opinion he didn't like them much either, apart from André who was OK, a bit *pantouflard* perhaps and with some really *weird* ideas. Jean-Pierre Beltoise? That one? *Oh-là-là, un vrai avorton.* Otherwise André was a good sort, *un bon vieux.*

'*Un bon vieux?* I suppose you liked his paintings too. They're shit as far as I'm concerned. *Merde, merde, merde, merde.*' I was crying now, crying because they had laughed at him, at me, and because Georges hadn't the guts to retaliate. He patted me awkwardly on the back. 'They're really not worth it,' he repeated, 'not worth it at all.'

'Don't you understand – they're my *life*. Of course they're worth it.'

'But, Janey, Rachel is your friend, yes. The others – you don't know them from Adam.'

'Where were you, Adam?' I hissed at him through my teeth. '*Eine Weltkatastrophe kann zu manchem dienen.*'

'Adam who?'

'*Auch dazu, ein Alibi zu finden vor Gott.* Where were you, Adam? "I was in the World War". Heinrich Böll. German.'

'Ah, German. *J'aime pas les Boches.*'

'War is a sickness, like typhoid.'

'Is that German too?'

'Antoine de Saint-Exupéry. French if you didn't know. They're from the same book. Epigrams. No, what d'you call them? Epigraphs.'

'Listen, Janey, I don't understand what you're trying to say.'

'That's just it. You–don't–damn–well–understand.'

He looked small and lost, dragging one foot against the kerb. My anger slid away. It wasn't his fault our reading lists diverged, that he talked cars while Yves talked clouds.

'I'm sorry. They made me mad back there – Rachel and Hélène especially. Not Yves, I liked him.'

'So I noticed.'

'Don't start on that, please. I've had enough for one night. Let's go home.'

From several flights up came the scratching of a tinny radio. A woman's voice shouting, *Tais-toi, mon con.* Georges put his hands in his pockets, an expression of mild bewilderment on his face.

'There is just one problem,' he said, looking round at the greasy walls of the alley. 'You walked so fast, I couldn't keep track. Do you happen to know where we are?'

'Not a clue.'

'Then, Janey, unless we find the car, we are really *foutus.*'

It had started to rain. The cars were much less frequent now, headlights swooping out of the dark, vanishing with a whoosh of tyres on wet roads. Soon there was no one left but us. Maybe I slept. I had no idea what road we travelled or when our journey would end. The city had come to an abrupt halt as if we had passed from one zone to another and here we journeyed on our own, thundering through straggling villages that looked forlorn and uninhabited in the quickening rain. Georges held my hand as he drove, the other on the wheel. Once or twice he looked at me, neither happy nor sad, the face of a man who sees the flood waters recede and counts himself among the saved.

Though we had planned to stay several days in the city I was glad we were going home. Neither would mention this visit again, I was certain of that. It would become a tiny gap in our lives, thirty-six hours that had never happened. Resting my head on his shoulder I felt snug and safe, lulled by the rhythmic splashing of windscreen wipers and the blackness out there.

I was dozing when I felt the car pull off the road. After bumping along a track, the engine stopped and Georges got out. His hair was soaked when he came back inside, and his clothes, some of which he removed. We huddled together on the front seats under a blanket he had retrieved from the boot.

After a time you don't notice the rain clattering down on the tinny roof. You don't notice anything at all except the man who holds you in his arms, smelling of damp dog, who seems to be able to doze and stroke your hair at the same time, who doesn't say much – there isn't much to say.

Some time in the night the rain stopped. Everything went still. Before long it started to rain again. Then it stopped. And so it went on. It seemed a very long night.

This time I was the one to wake first in the grey light of morning, feeling as if someone had tied me up with string. My arms ached. My shoulder ached. My back was twisted like a corkscrew, one foot wedged under the seat. Georges had managed to steal most of the blanket and was sleeping in a tight ball by the door. I climbed out as quietly as I could and went to pee in the bushes. Vegetation dripped all around. My shoes sank in the mud. I wondered if we had any newspaper in the car.

Georges was stirring when I returned. We kissed through the open window. Unshaven, he looked very old. Puckered eyes from staring too hard at the sun.

'I want to talk to you.'

'OK.' I got in the car.

Georges didn't speak straight away. Didn't touch me either. I felt numb at the prospect of what he was about to say and wished suddenly that I was far away.

'I want us to marry,' he said at last. 'You know that, don't you?'

I held my breath and prayed.

'Let's do it when we get back. It won't take long to arrange. Unless you need to ask permission, from your parents, I mean.'

'But why the . . . hurry? I've got another year to complete. Why don't we do it then? I wouldn't want to marry you one day and go away the next.'

'You wouldn't need to go away. You are studying French, no? Well, then. You'll be here. I'll teach you everything you need to know.'

The car was parked in a clearing surrounded by trees. In the distance, the track wound round to a small cottage, mean and grey. I felt my face going red.

'Please, Georges, don't think badly of me. I want to marry you very much, but later. I like to finish things once I've started them. I *have* to go back.'

'Then you will forget me,' he said, very matter-of-fact.

'That's not true. You know it isn't.'

'I know you better than you know yourself, remember.' I turned to look at him. His lips were smiling at me, even if his eyes weren't.

'I'll write to them tonight, my parents. I've already told them about you. They're probably expecting it.'

'What will you tell them?'

'That we'll marry next year. Here . . . in England, I don't know. We've ages to think of that. It's a promise, Georges, it really is. You don't answer. Don't you believe me?'

'Promises, promises, I know the value of those. I wish you hadn't said that, Janey. But if you say it's true, I must believe you. What choice do I have?'

Georges found the key in his pocket and started the engine. As we backed towards the road, tyres spinning in the mud, I thought fleetingly of Yves. I had always wanted to marry a writer. He had a quick gleam to his eye that made you feel special, clever and worldly wise. I heard the noise of doors banging shut. There was always the problem of Hélène, and Tolkien. Georges yawned as he drove, tapping his fingers on the steering wheel. Faith heals, I thought, makes you believe that what you want is possible. But what do *I* want? What do *I* dream? And if I knew the answer to that, is this the man who could make it come true? Is it? Is it?

EIGHT

I kept at least one of the promises I made to Georges that day: I wrote immediately to my parents, telling them of the man I had decided to marry and asking in a roundabout way for their approval. The news about Georges appeared towards the end after a sanitised version of my trip to Paris in which I travelled with Kate and stayed several days. I even mentioned the detour to Chartres, though as we had supposedly travelled by train the logistics of our journey are baffling, to say the least. I know this because I recently re-read the letter: Mum keeps everything I write neatly parcelled with rubber bands and stored beneath her bed in an old leather case. Reading the letters made me sad. Despite their arbitrary lies, the half-truths that can have fooled no one, they seem more painfully honest than the short brittle letters I write now.

> You will probably be very surprised to hear from me again so soon but I have suddenly realised why I have been so happy here and wanted you to be the first to know. It's Georges – the man I met at the Anglo-French Society. We've been seeing a lot of each other recently and what I thought was a very close friendship has turned into love on both sides. Auntie Bets always said I'd know when I met the right man: he'd make my hat fall off. I don't wear hats but I get that funny feeling in my stomach and all the

time I feel so incredibly surprised and astonished that it's happening to me. Don't be frightened for me. Though we'll have to spend a year apart while I finish my degree I know he'll be waiting for me and you don't hurt someone when you love them. Right from the start we seemed to get on so well and we love each other very much. He makes me happy and that's the main thing, isn't it?

There are a few things about him that might surprise you but once you've met him I know you'll like him as much as I do. (Well, maybe not quite!) I doubt if you could call him good-looking. He's about my height with curly black hair a bit like Martin's and eyes that crease up when he smiles. You'll be pleased to know, Dad, that he often wears a suit and looks very good in it. At the moment he's Deputy Manager at Carrefour, one of the largest supermarket chains in France, but he's not very happy as he objects to being called a grocer so he's looking for something else. I think I've already told you that he plays the guitar and sings in a voice that sounds like footsteps walking on gravel, if you know what I mean.

I should warn you that Georges is much older than I am – he's thirty-five – but when we're together the difference disappears. The fact that he's French and I'm English doesn't seem to matter either. Even when I express myself badly and get muddled up (which happens all the time) we always end up understanding each other. His father died a few years ago from cancer: a champion cyclist, so Georges says, though I'm not sure that's right. Now he lives with his mother (you can see how respectable he is) – I haven't met her yet. The French are far more formal than we are and it's quite an event when a girl is finally introduced to the parents. She worked for Shell and used to be an opera singer but has now retired. Her main hobby is birds. She feeds the pigeons that come to her window and has fourteen canaries.

There's still a lot to sort out. I've said we shouldn't get married until after I've sat my exams. Then I suppose we'll live in France, in Bordeaux to begin with, though Georges plans to move north later on. Don't be sad. I'll come over for holidays as often as I can and you'll come here. Please write and tell me that you don't mind – I wish you could meet him right away so that you would know I really am doing the right thing, for once. Till soon and much love – Janey.

PS Georges's surname is DELVAUX. I didn't know that myself straightaway as it never occurred to me to ask until we went to a party and I had to introduce him to some French friends. You should have seen their faces when I had to ask him his name, in front of everyone, and it was obvious we knew each other very well.

They replied by return or rather Dad did, giving his 'permission'. Normally he leaves letter-writing to Mum but the granting of a daughter's hand in marriage was man's work, I suppose. Mum added a postscript saying that fifteen years age difference wasn't too much of a handicap as long as we both knew what we were doing and could I please send a photograph of Georges which she could show to her friends, to Maureen and Auntie Bets? Their approval sounded genuine: I was surprised, alarmed even by the extent of their trust in me but I knew Georges and they didn't.

I showed him Dad's letter, translating every word apart from the reference to his job at Carrefour. (Dad thought the title of Deputy Manager more than compensated for being called a grocer.) Georges looked pleased.

'They sound nice, your parents.'

'They are.'

'So, Madame Future-Delvaux,' he said, kissing me in the café and slipping his tongue between my teeth, 'you may meet the other one now.'

71

'Your mother? Oh Georges, I bet she doesn't even know I exist.'

'Of course she knows all about you, *ma fleur*. I have told her everything.'

'About my lips, my sex, my *ligne de hanches*?'

'Those are secrets, Mademoiselle, for you and me alone.' He ran his hand down the bump of my nose and across my half-open lips. It made me feel warm inside. 'But she couldn't meet you until your parents had given their permission. She wouldn't want to condone an engagement of which they might disapprove.'

'You can't be serious.'

'*Mais c'est normal.*'

'Not with me it isn't.'

'Wait till you meet my mother. Then you will see what a dragon she is for the proprieties.'

It wasn't long before I understood what he meant. As soon as Madame was informed of my father's written approval she extended a gracious invitation to meet, not at home – that, apparently, had to wait until we were better acquainted. No, the three of us would take Sunday lunch at a country inn on the banks of the Garonne that promised peace, tranquillity and good bourgeois food. I had to borrow a decent skirt from Kate and took my one sober shirt to the *pressing* round the corner. At the last minute I bought a hair band to complete the right impression.

Monsieur Gilbert came running over himself to tell me the car was waiting at the gate. At the summer-house door he tucked his beret under his arm and gave me a military bow, the kind usually reserved for Kate. Having spied the august presence of Madame Delvaux he must have revised his opinion of my character and offered to accompany me to the road.

'A beautiful day for an outing, don't you think, Mademoiselle? I am taking Madame Gilbert to see my niece. Her husband owns a vineyard near Libourne. I shall bring you back some wine . . . *le plus bong*.' He kissed his fingers to the air.

At the gate he gave me another bow and took my hand, holding it longer than was strictly correct. I wondered if Madame Delvaux was watching us from the car.

Kate's skirt snagged on the door handle as I climbed into the back. Instead of his usual kiss, Georges winked at me over his shoulder. Madame turned round, majestically offering her hand.

'So you are Janey.' Her careful inspection made the blood rise to my cheeks. 'Georges has told me all about you.'

'Good things, I hope.' My laughter sounded cracked.

She didn't smile but behind her mask of severity I detected a small measure of warmth.

Georges started the engine and we drove sedately out of the city. Madame kept her eyes on the road. From the back seat I was able to inspect her unobserved. One of her bra straps hung loose. She had a fleshy opera–singer's neck with a fine head of blonde hair swept up into a chignon. Georges must take after his father, the champion cyclist, because there was nothing, absolutely nothing to link him to this terrifying female who moved like a ship through water without bending her head. She and Georges spoke occasionally in lowered tones.

The distance enforced by his mother's presence drove me insane. By the time we arrived at the vine-covered inn I was feeling distinctly queasy. As Georges helped me out of the car he said my hands felt damp.

'Cheer up, it isn't that bad. I think she likes you.'

'Does she really? I like her too, I think. But I'm horribly nervous.'

He kissed my earlobe while Madame advanced up the path.

We were shown to a table outside by the riverbank. I was given the chair that faced directly into the sun. If Madame noticed my discomfort she made no offer to adjust the seating.

I warmed to her all the same. Most of her conversation centred on my family: what my father did, the kind of people we knew, my mother's connections and what my younger brother planned to do. I explained that as Martin was only sixteen he hadn't yet made up his mind or if he had, he hadn't bothered to let anyone know.

'Surely your parents have made it their business to enquire?'

'Not necessarily. He's very happy-go-lucky, my brother, I suppose because he's the youngest. He does OK at school, when he puts his mind to it. Mum and Dad know that he'll find out what he wants to do, one day, and they're happy to leave it at that.'

Her eyebrows rose fractionally. 'They sound very modern, your parents.'

The sunlight made my head ache. I looked at Georges for support. He said, 'Not modern, *Maman*. They do things differently in England.'

'So I see. But you, child,' she said, smiling at me for the first time, 'shall become one of us.'

Georges leaned back in his chair and lit a cigarette. I could tell he was pleased. It seemed daft that a grown man should worry what his mother thought of his intended bride but I had worried too and despised myself for caring one way

74

or the other. If she didn't like me that was her problem: I wasn't marrying her.

Conversation was halted by the arrival of a lugubrious waiter called Paul who muttered and wheezed as he staggered down the path bearing platefuls of food. To my relief Madame preferred eating to talking. We started with *foie de canard aux raisins*, progressed to a simple *poulet grillé aux sarments*, ate our way through a mound of floury potatoes cooked in goose fat and ended with a refreshingly light *oeufs à la neige*. My head began to buzz from too much sun and the heavy red wine that Georges kept pouring into my glass. He shouted at Paul to bring another bottle.

'I think we have had enough already,' said Madame, wiping a smear of grease from her powdered cheek.

'Nonsense, *Maman*, just one more.'

Georges had gone inside to order coffee, leaving the two of us alone. I listened to the gurgling of the river punctured by raucous laughter at a nearby table from which the youngest members of a very extended family overspilled on to the grass. Babies, cousins, uncles, aunts, a whole fleet of grandmothers: they sounded very jolly. The men had removed their jackets as the wine continued to flow.

Escaping from its companions, one of the toddlers lurched in our direction.

'You like children?' asked Madame Delvaux, noting my momentary look of alarm.

'Er, yes . . . very much.'

Madame held out her hands to the tottering child. The boy – or girl – wrinkled its stubby nose then started to wail.

'You know Georges has a son. He told you that, didn't he?'

My spoon bounced off the plate, leaving a sticky stain in the lap of Kate's skirt before skidding on to the ground. As I bent down under the table I saw that Madame had removed both shoes.

'He told me that, yes. Pascal, isn't it?'

'What else did he tell you?'

'That he doesn't see the boy any more. It seems terribly sad.'

'Not that.' She shook her head impatiently. 'Surely he has told you what happened?'

'Madame, I'm afraid I don't know what you mean. He's told me lots of things. What exactly . . .'

She made a sort of tutting noise and would have told me, I'm sure, had not Georges suddenly returned. He stood behind his chair, looking sharply at me.

'Janey and I were talking,' said his mother. 'It seems you have left her in the dark. You know, Georges, that really isn't right. If she is to become your wife she must be told the facts, it's only fair. Otherwise she won't know what sort of a bargain she has made.'

'She knows,' he said curtly.

'I'm not sure she does. You cannot expect miracles, my son. We have talked of this before. The past won't go away, you know, but if you face up to what has happened, face up to it like a man, well . . .'

'*Maman*, please don't spoil our day together. We have enjoyed our lunch very much – you couldn't have done better yourself. Janey and I understand each other well. When I tell you that she knows, I mean exactly that.'

He sat down breathing heavily and quickly drained his glass. Madame drummed her plump fingers on the tablecloth. The sun had disappeared behind a cloud. I said, 'Yes, we really did enjoy the meal. It's the best

I've had in ages. But if there's something I should know . . .'

Georges cut straight across me. 'I had a word with Monsieur Duhamel inside. He asked after you, *Maman*, so I gave him your compliments. Look, he's coming here now. He says he hasn't seen you in months.'

Madame's hands strayed to her chignon, replacing the odd stray hair, then her head turned slowly on its axis as the *patron* – all black-and-white – waddled like a penguin through the grass. Georges stood up. I felt confused by the sudden change in their relationship: when Georges said no, flatly and firmly, his mother did as she was told. The rest of the time he danced attendance on her. It was as if each had some hold over the other. As for the thing I was or was not supposed to know . . . I was beginning to get annoyed.

The penguin stopped at our table, rocking back and forwards on his flat feet. In a kittenish voice Madame repeated her compliments on the excellence of our meal.

'Just a simple table,' said Monsieur Duhamel, smirking.

'Simplicity is the hardest virtue to achieve.'

'Like lilies in the field. I know the values that my customers appreciate.'

'You pay us the compliment of choosing well.'

Georges sat down and reached for my hand under the tablecloth.

'We are here for a very special reason,' announced Madame Delvaux, smiling at the *patron* whose face registered rapt attention, bushy eyebrows raised. The waiter who plays at being a waiter. Jean-Paul Sartre, *Being and Nothingness*. I understood in a flash what he meant. 'I would like to present my daughter-in-law, my future daughter-in-law. She and Georges are to marry next year. Mademoiselle Janey, may I introduce you to our host, Monsieur Duhamel, a very dear friend.'

'*Enchanté, Mademoiselle.*' He clapped his hands. '*Magnifique.*' Georges offered him the seat next to me. He sat down without releasing me from his glance then unexpectedly slapped Georges hard on the back. '*Ouff, mon brave.* Lucky man. If I were only younger myself.'

His oily stare made me jam my legs together. Georges and his mother regarded me with obvious satisfaction as if I had just secured First Prize at the show. My forced smile veered towards a frown. Monsieur Duhamel shook his head: it made his cheeks wobble. I noticed the greyish roots of his raven–black hair.

'Madame,' he said, still gargling a mouthful of marbles, 'this calls for a celebration. First, that you have graced my table again after your protracted absence. I thought you had deserted us.' She puckered her lips in protest. 'And second, that you bring me this ravishing creature. Georges, fetch us the brandy, will you? Unless you prefer champagne?' He looked first at me then at her. Madame said brandy would be excellent.

'Mind you bring the best,' he said to Georges, passing him a thick bunch of keys. 'Ask Paul to find you the Armagnac. Five star.' He leant towards Madame. 'I keep it locked away. With staff these days you need a Gorgon's eyes.' He raised his bushy eyebrows to the sky.

Their conversation continued above my head in sallies of elaborate courtesies batted back and forth like a shuttlecock. More than once I caught Monsieur Duhamel's glance creeping up my legs and was glad of Kate's skirt. He asked if I liked Bordeaux and answered the question himself: 'Of course you do. Otherwise you would not choose to remain. Is that not so, Mademoiselle?'

Georges returned, followed at a distance by Paul, still muttering to himself, who held out the brandy bottle on a silver tray. After banging the glasses down on the table, he passed the bottle and the keys to the *patron* and stood panting behind his boss's chair.

Before we could drink, Monsieur Duhamel was called away to say goodbye to the large family party who straggled towards the *parking*. A tiny girl, her hair bunched into a Chinese topknot, turned an awkward somersault on the grass. He slid forward to pick her up. As he set her on her feet I noticed his hand gliding down the curves of her infant bottom, coming to rest between her chubby thighs.

His duties as host fulfilled, we toasted the happy couple, the return of Madame Delvaux, the prosperity of Monsieur Duhamel's business and the expected arrival of a new generation of little Delvaux. After wine, the brandy went straight to my head and I felt myself turning pink.

The brownish waters of the river felt shockingly cold. Slime oozed between my toes, fat pink toes that sank into the mud of the riverbed. Long-legged insects skimmed across the water's surface, dappled with light and shade. Sounds pure as air: the slow sweep of the river, constant chirpings and twitterings, never still, a distant rumble of thunder or maybe a waterfall downstream. 'Look, Georges, fish, you can see them everywhere.' He found a stick and together we bent over the water, poking at shoals of silvery fish that darted in tight formation among the reeds. The *patron* had taken my seat next to Georges's mother. They watched us from the bank. When Georges touched my hand I felt my body stiffen. 'Watch out,' he called – I nearly fell – and as his arms closed around me I wished with all my heart that we had come here alone.

★   ★   ★

Georges dropped his mother off first. On the street outside her apartment we said goodbye in a flurry of 'thank yous' and repeated hopes that we should see each other soon. I moved to kiss her but she had already turned aside. Then he drove me home. From the open garage doors I knew that the Gilberts had not yet returned from Libourne.

'Georges,' I said, feeling reckless, 'why don't you come in, just for a minute. The Gilberts are spending the day with their niece. The old man told me himself this morning. They'll not be back for hours. I know Kate would like to see you.'

He looked doubtful. 'What will the neighbours say?'

'Come on, we'll not stay long.'

Hand in hand we ducked through the gate and ran up the path. The door to the summer-house was locked. So Kate was out too. I hadn't expected that. In my haste to find the key I emptied my bag on the step. Georges hid his face among the rose trees. As soon as I had opened the door we slipped inside. Click-click went the lock. The scrape of bolts being drawn.

The house was very quiet. Too quiet. I found a note from Kate on top of my class books. *Jules et Jim* was playing at a cinema in town. She was going with some of the others – didn't know when she would be back. Georges tried to kiss me against the door and looked annoyed when I pushed him away.

'What's the matter with you?'

'I shouldn't have asked you in. The Gilberts would kill me if they found out.'

'I think you exaggerate, *ma chérie*. No one can see us here. Ten minutes, that's all I ask: you won't begrudge me that?'

He was studying my sketches on the wall. There were

80

several of Kate, one of Bertrand asleep in the dunes and at least a dozen of Georges. 'Not bad,' he said, 'though I prefer the one you gave me. Sacred Monsters, you remember.'

'Take the lot if you want, but you really must go.'

'What's the fuss? Give me some tea and then I'll leave.' I shook my head vigorously. 'But you surely have tea – you are English, *non*? One good cup of tea and then I'll go. And while I wait,' he said, winking, 'I shall inspect the famous sausage.'

He went into the bedroom. I put a saucepan of water on the stove then stood sentinel by the door, peering through the net curtain. The neighbouring gardens dozed in the late afternoon heat. Distant lawnmower sounds. A car moving off down the street.

I heard him walking round the room, the creak of bedsprings. What's he doing in there, for God's sake? We should have driven out of town. There were any number of places where we could count on a minimum of privacy. Anywhere but here. The water began to knock and bubble in the pan. I turned down the gas. This was stupid. Get him out of here, fast. If he crept behind the bower then ran across the lawn he would reach the mimosa bushes in about five seconds. From there he could slip between the trees on the far boundary . . .

A noise made me turn round. Georges was standing in the bedroom doorway, the buttons of his shirt undone. Starched white shirt like the penguin's. He must have left his jacket in the other room. That look in his eyes. It said: don't pretend this isn't why you asked me in.

I felt my hat fall off.

The bedroom was dark. Slatted light from the shutters. He pulled me down on top of him. Kate's skirt got in the way.

His hands reaching for the zip. He slid it over my knees then tossed it across the room. It caught on the chair. Georges himself stayed in his clothes. I felt the sharp metal of his buckle between my legs. Cried out in pleasure, not pain.

Like sex in the car it didn't take long, our sense of danger heightened by a shared understanding – however fleeting – of the fragility of those emotions we called 'love' because we didn't know what else they might be. Expert hands parted my underclothes. A fumbling of fingers as he sought to connect then a sliding fullness that triggered a sound deep in my throat. For the first time he left off his *capote anglaise*. I think he asked me if I minded. I couldn't say no. We wanted children, lots of them. He didn't know I was taking the Pill. It happened so fast and I certainly hadn't intended to lie.

The minutes ticked past. Time had developed the quality of elastic. I noticed the bars of light from the shutters had gone. The room looked darker, fuzzier.

'Georges, you must leave. Now. This minute.'

'Don't want to,' he said sleepily. 'I want to stay for ever. Till morning, at least.'

'You can't. Kate will be back soon, and the Gilberts.'

'She might like it, just the three of us.'

'Don't be silly.'

'How do you know if you don't ask?'

'Well, I wouldn't like it and I'm not going to ask now.'

When I came back from the bathroom, a towel around my waist, I found Georges had crawled between the sheets, his head poking out at one end like a furry black animal. Men when they sleep: there's something soft and helpless about them. I wandered round the room picking up discarded clothes then sat on the edge of the bed, my hand resting on the mound of bedclothes that rose and fell as he breathed. A scraping of crickets outside. He smiled dreamily as I stroked the back of his head, curling the dark ends of his hair around my fingers and fighting the temptation to climb between the sheets and fall asleep too.

On the point of shaking him awake I saw a shadow pass in front of the shutters. A man's shadow. I knew it wasn't Kate. She's taller than that and takes a shorter route across the lawn. Monsieur Gilbert, it had to be. No one else would come.

Loud knocking at the door.

'Mademoiselle, open up at once. That man of yours – I know he's in there. I have seen his car parked in the street.'

Georges, startled awake, sat up in bed. At least he was dressed. I leapt across the room to the chair and jumped feet-first into Kate's skirt that was hanging off the side. The skirt was upside-down. I tried again. More knocking at the door. I managed to fasten the zip but heard a ripping sound as I straightened the seams.

'*J'arrive*, Monsieur, one moment. I can explain every-thing.'

Leaving Georges in the bedroom I ran through to the kitchen. There was a slight smell of gas. I must have left it on. The lock was holding, just, but Monsieur Gilbert was pushing hard from the other side, rattling the glass panels so fiercely I was frightened it might explode in my face.

The key had fallen out of the lock. I fumbled for it on the floor. It slipped away from my fingers like soap. His knocking and rattling continued at full strength.

As I pushed aside the curtain to unlock the door our eyes met through the glass. Beneath the beret his face looked incandescent with rage.

'Open up, I say.'

I turned the key in the lock. There was a moment's calm. Monsieur Gilbert straightened up. Georges moved into the room behind me, to give me courage, I think. Then I pulled back the bolts and opened the door.

Monsieur Gilbert stumbled as he stepped backwards into the flowerbeds. 'Come outside,' he ordered. 'You, Mademoiselle, and you . . . He thrust his purple face at Georges.

We went through the door together and stood like wayward children on the gravel. The old man gripped a wine bottle by the throat. He was waving it around. I stepped between the two men.

'Please, Monsieur. It's not what you think. Georges, Monsieur Delvaux, was helping me with an essay. We've been out for the day, with his mother. You saw her, I think, this morning.'

Mothers and rage collided with a crunch.

'With his mother . . . With his mother . . . This is an outrage. How dare you, the pair of you? I put my faith in you, Mademoiselle, my faith. You have dishonoured my name, my trust, my wife, *la pauvre sainte*' – he crossed himself hurriedly – 'here in my property. And now you dare to drag his mother into this?'

'Yes, but you see, the essay. We were out so long, I didn't have time . . .'

His eyes dropped to our feet on the path. 'You write an essay without shoes? Helped by a man who has also decided to remove his shoes? *Pour mieux se concentrer, c'est ça?* I don't believe a word, *pas-un-seul-mot*. Your conduct is a disgrace to the honour of the university. Your professors will hear of this. I shall tell them everything.'

Brandishing his niece's wine bottle he advanced towards

84

Georges who ducked behind my back. He would have hit me gladly if I came in the way. I glanced towards the house. Madame Gilbert, at the window, had covered her face with her hands.

I heard the gate clang.

Kate started to wave. When she saw Georges her hand dropped to her side.

'Look,' I shouted, 'there's Kate.'

Monsieur Gilbert, still swinging his bottle, turned round.

'Run,' I hissed to Georges. 'I'll handle this one.'

Without further encouragement he sped shoeless across the lawn, clearing the flowerbeds in a single leap and careering past Kate who turned as he vaulted over the gate and disappeared into the street. A few seconds later we heard the engine kick into life. The squeal of tyres reversing at speed.

Though I had told him to run, his flight disappointed me. I hadn't meant him to abandon me so completely. Monsieur Gilbert dropped his arm. He held the bottle like a meat cleaver, too angry to speak. As he marched back towards the house I heard him muttering wildly to himself. *La pute*, I think he said. He made it sound like spit.

On the steps to the house he turned and shouted across the garden, 'You will wait in the summer-house. I must now confer with Madame, my wife. We shall inform you what action we intend to take. Good day.'

Kate came running over. I was trembling so much she had to help me inside.

'What'll he do to me?'

'He won't let you stay, that's certain, not after this. I don't see what else he can do.'

'He said he was going to talk to my tutors.'

'I expect he will but there's no law against it. They can't kick you out for this.'

'Where will I live?'

'Georges has friends, doesn't he? He's bound to be able to fix you up with a room somewhere. It won't be for long. We've only got a few weeks left.'

'Kate, I'm sorry. Do you think he'll make you go too?'

'We'll have to wait and see. You said he was going to speak to his wife. Maybe she'll put in a good word for us.'

'No chance there. I'm sure she disapproves even more than he does. All the time I see her watching from the house. The old bag has been waiting for something like this to happen.'

'Well, you did rather hand it to them . . .'

Kate went to bed after we had talked for some time. I packed my things as quietly as I could, including Georges's shoes, returned Kate's skirt (the seam had ripped, nothing serious, and I managed to remove the lunch stains under the tap), then I sat and waited for Monsieur Gilbert's inevitable dismissal. Looking around the tidy kitchen, my sketches taken down from the walls, I knew I would miss the place, its *camping-gaz* smell, Kate and the sausage, the sense of order it gave to my otherwise unruly life.

I had asked him inside. He came and we ended up in bed. Surprise, surprise. I couldn't blame him.

I was almost relieved when, around 10.30 p.m., I heard the crunch of footsteps on gravel. *Bon courage*, I whispered as Monsieur Gilbert's shadow paused outside the door. He bent down. A large white envelope appeared through the bottom gap. I took it while he was still pushing from the other side and read the brief résumé of his *conseil* with

Madame Gilbert. For reasons that would be entirely clear to the recipient it was formally requested that Mademoiselle Wilcox should vacate the summer-house by 10 a.m. the following day. As an entirely blameless party Mademoiselle Gardner (Kate) was welcome and indeed warmly pressed to remain. She brought such pleasure to their lives; they would not wish to see her go. Assuring you, Mademoiselle, of the dignity of our best sentiments et cetera.

I gave the old man time to return to the house then went out to telephone Georges, something I had never done before. We always fixed a time and place before we said goodbye. His mother answered the phone after I had let it ring for some time. Again, I thanked her for her hospitality. She thanked me for calling: said it restored her faith in the good manners of the young even if the hour was somewhat late.

Towards the end of our conversation I asked – casually – if Georges was home. She said he had returned briefly a while ago but had then gone out again.

'Perhaps you have a message you would like me to pass on?'

'You don't know where he is, I suppose?'

'I'm afraid not. Georges never says where he goes. But he's not with you? I must say, I had wondered. *Bon*. Perhaps when I see him tomorrow I can tell him . . .'

'No message,' I said quickly. 'It was just a thought. I'll tell him when I next see him. Really.'

'As you like.'

I cursed him when I put down the phone, wondering what on earth I should do when morning came.

NINE

I went to Carrefour, that's what I did, lugging my suitcase on and off the bus then into a trolley which I wheeled disconsolately around the supermarket shelves. At last I spied a familiar white-coated figure disappearing behind the tinned fruit, not Georges but his friend Bertrand whom I had last seen at the car rally where we made up a four with Kate. The rally marked the end of their brief liaison. Lured along forest tracks by the devious misdirections of a wily old peasant, Bertrand had innocently joked that he and Georges would abandon us both unless Kate and I agreed to drop our knickers, *faire zizi-panpan*. Kate had slapped his face and said she never wanted to go with him again. I liked him, actually. He was younger than Georges, just a few years older than I, and played a passable buffoon.

As I ran after him, my suitcase piled in the trolley, I took the corner badly and skidded broadside into a couple of frail and very elderly women, one of whom landed with a loud thump on the tiles, dumpy legs out-stretched, a pair of stockings rolled up to her knees. I was just attempting to extricate the old woman's stick when Bertrand bustled over from the tinned fruit section. He helped her to her feet, all the time glaring at me with contempt.

'Don't worry, Mesdames,' he said, grabbing hold of my

elbow, 'I shall take her to the manager. He will deal with this . . . this *andouille*.'

He propelled me forwards. With only one free hand, I managed to steer my trolley into a pillar, dislodging chunks of plaster.

'Well, really,' he fumed, 'you need a licence before you enter these premises again. I drive, now.' Raising his white cap to the women, he set off towards the far end. I had to run to keep pace with him. Then he sidestepped into an aisle and kissed me quickly on the cheeks.

'Trouble, eh?' he asked, pointing at the suitcase.

'I'm afraid so. Is Georges here? I need to see him at once.'

Bertrand shook his head. My heart sank.

'Where is he?'

'Oh, he's here all right. Only, he can't see you right now. This morning, he came in very late. Almost an hour late. The manager called him into his office. That made him later still. You should have heard them inside: *bif, baf, ouff*. What were you doing, the pair of you? Georges said you go like a *bombe* but this is ridiculous. He looked shagged out. I had to lend him a razor.'

Bertrand started waving his arms at me: 'You are very clumsy, Mademoiselle. One day you will kill someone. I put my money on it, if I had any. The manager is not here, right now, otherwise he would hand you over to the authorities. They know how to deal with people like you.'

I followed the line of his eye.

Two heads had appeared round the side of the aisle.

I tried to say I was sorry.

'That is not enough. Come with me.'

He walked back towards the two women. I followed

meekly in his wake, alarmed to notice that we were heading towards the check-outs.

'Bertrand, you must help me. I have to speak with Georges.'

He looked quickly to left and right. 'You need somewhere to put that, don't you? I'll tell you what I'll do. Georges can't come right now, not unless he wants another kick up the pants. He had to forfeit all his breaks, today and tomorrow. But I will find him and get the keys for you, the keys to the car. Assuming that he came by car. A breakdown would have explained everything. The manager has problems in that department himself but then he buys a Jaguar. *Bof.* Wait over there.'

He nodded towards the meat counter where a queue had started to form. I joined the end of it, several times almost reaching the front.

It seemed ages before Bertrand reappeared, tiptoeing between the aisles. 'Georges sends his love. He was sorry to hear about that.' He nodded at the suitcase and gave me a conspiratorial wink. 'I understand you put up quite a show. Jolly good. Let the old geese go shit themselves. *Elles sont toutes des dames-pipi.* But here are the keys. The car is round the side, in the staff *parking.* If anyone stops you, don't mention Georges's name. He's in enough trouble already.'

'How shall I get the keys back to him? Will you be here?'

'No, I have things to do. Hide the keys in the car. I'll tell Georges.'

'But that'll mean leaving it unlocked. My things . . .'

Bertrand looked impatient. 'I cannot think of everything,' he said.

After I had found the car I heaved my suitcase into the boot which already contained several packages concealed in bundles of old newspaper. I wasn't sure what to do next. In class, it was my turn to lead the discussion. I hadn't read the books, nor had I started the essay which I was supposed to read out loud. Even if I caught a bus now, I was bound to miss the beginning. The thought of more excuses, more lies, switched off what little sense of responsibility remained. I climbed into the back first, thinking I might sleep, but it felt cramped so I changed places for the passenger seat in front, smoking the last of my cigarettes and imagining the look on Georges's face when he discovered I had waited for him patiently all day.

As time dragged on I counted the people who entered the building through the staff door, the ones who left, and then I counted birds in the sky. Once I went inside to buy some bread and find a bathroom I could use and though I hunted the aisles for sight of Bertrand or Georges I saw no one I knew.

It was dusk before Georges appeared at the exit. After glancing at the sky he walked towards the car where he stood by the door, searching his pockets for the keys. He looked startled when I leant across the driver's seat to open the door. Then he saw who it was and sat down heavily beside me, burying his head on my shoulder.

We ate in the café near the docks then cruised the port, stopping in front of a succession of café-bars lining the *quais*. He appeared to be searching for someone. Once he went inside, leaving me behind in the car. The streets were deserted. A couple of gendarmes passed. They halted by the car, squatting down on the pavement to look at me through the side windows. They were still leaning against the car when Georges re-emerged from the bar. He greeted them like friends. Inside the car he put his hand between my legs and kissed my neck. That sudden kick of desire. I moved to accommodate him but the car was parked underneath a streetlamp which turned our faces a ghostly orange, and the flesh of my thighs. Looking over my shoulder, I saw the gendarmes saluting at Georges as we drove away.

I didn't recognise the street. The once elegant *quartier* stank of neglect. Crumbling villas set in cracked concrete and weeds. Even the streetlamps were sparse, hoarding their circles of light that magnified the blackness beyond.

Georges was gone for some time. How long I didn't know: I wasn't keeping count. The car had become my home, a place where time lost its edge. Inside its tinny walls I felt safe, safer than the houses out there as long as I stayed where I was.

The villa door opened. Georges appeared at the top of the steps followed by a dark shape I first mistook for his shadow. The house had no light in any of its windows. It looked as empty as the rest.

He seemed to be waving me in. Reluctantly I opened the door and hesitated before walking quickly towards the house. The echo of my footsteps frightened me.

He came down the steps to meet me. 'You can stay here,' he said. 'Don't worry, it's not as bad as it looks. Jean will let you have a room at the front.'

'Jean?'

The big man disengaged himself from the shadows and offered me his hand, pink and fleshed like a butcher's with a grip to match. I couldn't see his face, just the broken angle of his nose, a full head of hair, thick and straight. He looked altogether larger than my first impression, that

92

day in the café, but gentler, too. I thought: maybe he's not so bad after all.

Georges said, 'No electricity, I'm afraid. There's running water at least, and candles. Sylvie will show you in the morning.'

'Sylvie is your wife?' I asked, I don't know why.

A woman's voice called from behind the partition, a strident voice with an accent I couldn't place. French, undoubtedly, but from where? It said, 'Wives don't dare show their faces in this shit-hole.'

'Come, I'll show you the room,' said Georges, taking a lighted candle from a chair in the hall and shutting the door behind us.

The walls were parchment thin. Sylvie continued to screech at Jean on the other side. He sounded like a man who held his temper well.

By the light of a single candle it was hard to get the measure of my new home. The room looked like a storehouse: wooden crates by the wall, an upended chair, more packages like the ones I'd seen in Georges's car, rolled-up mattress on the floor. The shutters to the street were drawn. A second window to one side, hung with a blanket, let in a faint glow from the lights outside.

Georges put the candle down on the floor. 'It's the best I can do,' he said wearily. 'I'll get your things.'

Alone, I circled the walls. The crates were all nailed down. The wood was rough: it made my fingers bleed.

When Georges returned with my case we spread out the mattress together. It was thin and lumpy, stained in all the usual places. Instead of sheets he jerked the blanket down from the window, creating thick clouds of dust that made us cough. Without looking at me he started to undress,

93

down to underpants. I wasn't sure I wanted to, but did all the same.

Lay your clothes neatly in a pile – there on a crate. That's right. Leave your shoes till last. Don't know what you might find. Flies and spiders, dead or alive. Not damp, that's one thing. Dry as dust. And bones. Plenty of those here if you root around.

Georges watched me from the bed. Did I call it a bed? Slip of the tongue, really. You can accustom yourself to anything if you try hard enough. Even this.

Sylvie's screeching had subsided in the room next door, erupting as occasional shouts and slaps. I felt the walls were listening to us as we came together in the dark, seeking comfort from the familiar feel of each other's bodies in this derelict lodging house on the outskirts of town. I wanted him as much as I had ever done, from the day we had exchanged our first words on the jetty at Arcachon, only my mind had started to rebel, the voice that said this couldn't, wouldn't last.

Dust to dust and all that. *Shut up, said the night-watchman to the Pope, you sound like a vacuum cleaner.*

Georges sensed my discouragement. He was gentle and kind, folding me into his body as if, treated roughly, I might snap into so many pieces we would never be able to guess how they fitted back together again.

'Don't be sad.'
    'I'm not sad.'
    'But you are. Your cheeks are wet.'
    'It happens. You know how it is.'
    'Sure.'

94

'I've made a new resolution. I'm never going to cry again. Crying is for kids, anyway.'

Silence.

I closed my eyes as he stroked my hair. The room smelt of mushrooms, dry and rotten at the same time. Whenever I moved the rough blanket made my skin itch. My spirits sank into a hole. If Georges abandoned me, there was no one to whom I could turn: the woman looked a queer sort and while Big Jean might be less of an ogre than I had first assumed, he still didn't fit as a friend.

Only words could keep the fears at bay. Talking. Talking.

'What shall we do tomorrow?' I said, curling my hands around my lover's body, trying to ignore the lumps in the greasy mattress.

'We could go to the ocean, if you like. I don't know. *On verra.*'

We shall see.

I was tired of that.

'Listen, Georges,' I said, turning over on to my front. 'This place . . . I can't bear it. Let's go away, as far away from here as it is possible to go. Imagine. After a time we'd reach the ends of the earth, the point where the sea drops away and you find yourself falling into space. We'd be happy there, I know.'

'Just you and me, alone in the universe? Then what'd we do?'

'It wouldn't matter. On our own we could do what we liked. There'd be no one snooping at the door, no one to criticise the minute we do something wrong – they're driving me crazy. Don't you have dreams like that?'

'*Ah, tu sais* . . . my dreams are practical affairs. I think of what we shall do, how we shall build our lives together.

95

I dream of success, of hanging up my white coat for the last time and telling the manager to go hang himself.' He thumped the muscles of his raised forearm. 'But now I shall dream through you. Will you let me share them, your dreams? Just you and me in a great empty universe. I'll dream of you as a star, the brightest, craziest star of all, the one that carries on blinking when all the others die.'

'Stars die too?'

'Of course. By the time you see them in the sky they are mostly dead already.'

'I won't die.'

'Then you would be a miracle.'

'It happens.'

'If you believe enough, sure.'

My tears had gone. So had the tethers that held us to this horrible little room. He was taking me away as I had asked him to, far away from this city that sat on our spirits like a saucepan lid. I felt the brushing of wings, the strength in his arms that released me from the confines of my body, the paucity of its untried emotions, a lightness of touch down my spine, across the angle of my hips, my adolescent breasts, and there where I wanted him most, first his fingers then his tongue. Quick, darting movements like a dog's. My English boyfriends hadn't dared. He was different, this one: an older man who brought me forbidden joys, the tremor of his secret past, who served me his heart on a plate because that's what I wanted most, his severed heart still pumping on a silver tray while I, Salome, danced for the King. I was glad he couldn't see my face. My hands in his hair – stiff as a brush, it felt, and his voice calling through space, half-heard, half-felt, his voice that travelled faster than light from the embers of stars, *t'es complètement folle, mon petit Génie, ma bonne étoile, mon ange.*

TEN

That house: I thought of it the other day, smelt its reeking latrine in the back yard, heard the drip-drip-dripping of the cold-water tap in the room next to Sylvie's – the 'kitchen', she called it, laughing up her nose at my squeamish distaste for its bohemian squalor, a nesting for rats, cups and plates overspilling the cracked sink that sprouted fingers of green slime up bare-plastered walls. Someone had kicked down the doors separating the two rooms so you didn't enter the kitchen unless you were certain the house was empty because otherwise, God knows what you might find: Sylvie and Jean on all fours, most likely, mating like dogs or clawing at each other's throat. The difference was anyway slight.

I thought of Sylvie herself, the bloated bulge of her stomach, tight leather skirts and impossibly high-heeled shoes, her blue-veined legs mottled purple around the thighs; Sylvie who called me 'kid' and taught me how to give men what they wanted, a kick in the arse and the other thing too but drive them wild, first. Make the buggers pay was her philosophy and if they tried to sell you short, there were plenty of other fish to fuck in the sea. I thought of Jean retreating down the street, Sylvie in close pursuit, ducking the obscenities she hurled like missiles at his head. I thought of Georges (why do I always think of him?). It gave me such a pang I felt sick.

Lilies were the cause of my undoing.

It was half-term and Kate was coming to stay with the boys, Matthew (my godson), Frankie and little Sam. In anticipation of their visit, I was buying flowers in the village. Mary pointed out the lilies. Already opened, they would last a good few days. I could have them half-price, she said.

She had wrapped me two bunches before I had agreed to take them but I'm a good customer and she always knows what I like.

The bell went *tingaling*.

I looked down at the flowers pressed in my arms: lilies, white lilies (I don't know their name), Georges had brought me an armful that first day at the house, cast-offs from the cut-flower counter. I gave some to Sylvie who brandished them at Jean, calling him a mean-fisted bastard. Next time he waved his prick around she'd jam it in a vase instead. That heavy funereal scent, it made me feel giddy and faint.

'Are you all right?' asked Mary, her voice edged with concern.

'Thanks, Mary, I'll be fine.'

'Here, I'll get you some water, all the same,' she said, first pumping the door for air and setting off a frenzy of bells.

Back home, I arranged the flowers in two glass vases, one for the drawing-room mantelpiece, the other for a small mahogany table in the hall, opening all the windows to let the scent of lilies escape across the lawns.

And so I waited for Kate and the boys, curled up on

the big sofa Stephen kept in his office until his clients complained about the springs and asked jokingly if times were hard. Unable to part with its shabby gentility he persuaded me to find a corner for it in an alcove.

Then I think: this isn't real, Stephen, Kate, the boys, this comfortable house where every surface is polished, clean as a new pin, Mum would say, where every knick-knack has its place. The other – that was real. I can smell it even now, lilies and sweat, the fusty smell of sex, of semen and stained knickers, the crusted scabs of dirt that escaped my half-hearted attempts at cleanliness. Clean as pigs, Georges said or Saint-Exupéry's orientals *qui vivent dans la crasse et s'y plaisent*, though not being a literary man he didn't put it quite like that.

The day he brought me the lilies (our first full day in the house) we must have woken soon after dawn. Everything was tinged grey. Grey floors. Grey, peeling walls. Grey skin. Dirty grey blanket which Georges, as usual, had commandeered. Grey light seeping through the broken window to one side. Georges was stirring too, making snuffling noises as he opened his eyes. After he had kissed me, slipping his legs between mine and feeling for my sex, he looked at his watch.

'My God. Is that the time?'

He jumped up from the mattress and fumbled for his clothes, hopping around on one foot when the belt tangled on his trouser legs.

'Where are you going?'

'I go to work, what do you think? This is serious, you know. First I go home. I must shave, take a shower, change my clothes. I can't wear these, *ça pue*.'

'You said we'd go to the ocean. You *promised*.'

'Today is impossible. At the weekend, perhaps.'

'But what'll I do here on my own? I don't know where we are. I don't even know what day it is.'

'Tuesday. There's a bus quite close that will take you out to the campus. You can go to class. Here, I'll draw you a map.'

'Heading which way?'

He thought for a moment before holding out an arm. 'That way's west. It's not far.'

He came over to the mattress. I clung to his neck. He must have known how frightened I felt because he said, 'We'll find something better. Don't worry. This isn't for long.' I tried to hold him back but he prised himself free and left, slamming the front door behind him. The day yawned like an empty pit. I wondered what his mother would say when she saw the state he was in and hoped she wouldn't blame me.

I went to find the lavatory outside. Gruesome. At least with the door shut you could only guess at its more unpleasant secrets. After that I must have slept because when I next opened my eyes the sun shone directly through the window, bleeding into the greyness of my room. From the sounds next door it was obvious what Jean and Sylvie were doing. He grunted and slavered like a bear, every now and then banging against a hard object that skidded across the floor. Putting my hands over my ears only made it worse. Sylvie shouted at him, words I didn't know. A dictionary wouldn't have helped either, not with words like those.

I thought: are they doing this for my benefit, or have they forgotten I'm here? Something crashed into the wall and carried on crashing until the plaster started to shake.

I found some class books in my case and settled down to read, evidently with some success because I was not immediately aware of the silence that marked the end of their activities. It was soon replaced by fishwife screams from Sylvie who said she wasn't a fucking pin cushion (*ramasser des épingles*: it wasn't what I thought). She'd want good money for that.

After a time I heard his clumsy footsteps in the corridor, then the noise of the front door. You had to slam it hard to make it shut. Each time this happened, the house shook.

I wondered what time the bus left from the corner. Sylvie might know. There again, she might not. I decided not to ask, either way, and carried on with my book.

The door creaked open. I hadn't heard a knock. I jerked the blanket over my chest. Books clattered to the floor.

A girl, woman, stared at me from the doorway: Sylvie. Beneath her mauve-and-peach gown – it must have been stylish, once – you could see a grey slab of girdle and lumpish breasts.

'Hi, kid,' she said. 'Thought you might like this.' She passed me some fruit, a huge pimply orange. Then she noticed the books by my bed.

'Hope I'm not disturbing. Georges said you were serious. Eggheads, dickheads, all the same really. He's not bad, that one, not bad at all, but . . .' She shrugged.

'But what?'

'Never mind. You'll see. Men – what do you expect?' She called them something I didn't catch – *salopards*, I think, though it might have been worse. 'That one, Jean . . . He's now run snivelling to his wife. Next time he shows his face he can trim his own bloody wick, *se tailler la pipe soi-même*, or ask that fucking wife of his to oblige.'

101

She made a gesture with her hand then burst into tears. I didn't know what to do. Crying noisily, she wiped her face with the hem of her gown. I moved towards the wall to make space for her on the mattress.

'I thought he lived here. I mean, Georges told me this was his place.'

'It is.' She sniffed. 'He lives with her, too. She gets the bread, I get the prick and so much shit. Bad deal, what d'you think? Fucking bad deal. But then that's Jean for you.'

She sat up. Her eyes were dull as lead, her face welted with tears. 'If he wants to do business with you, no deal, understand?'

'What sort of business?'

'Any business. He deals, that's what Jean does.'

'Deals in what? Look, Sylvie, I don't understand.'

'You will. This and that. Not drugs, mind. He won't touch those. Just about everything else.' She sat with her legs apart, scratching one ankle with her toes. 'He'd pawn his grandmother if he thought anyone would want to dip his biscuit in that old bag.'

'If you think that Jean and I . . . There's Georges, remember. We're going to get married. Some time next year, probably.'

She laughed. I think she really found it funny. 'Make it quick,' she said, 'before he changes his mind. No, I don't mean that. You're not Jean's type. He screws like a greyhound then takes the stink back to that fancy bitch of his. Fuck knows what they get up to.'

Her gown open at the front, she lay back and stared at the ceiling. I started to peel the orange she had brought me. It tasted unnaturally sweet.

'I could quite take to that Georges of yours. He came after me once. I wasn't interested, then. Things change. I

102

hope he treats you well. When I knew him first, he was flat broke. Now that he's loaded I might change my mind.'

'I don't think he is. We neither of us have much money.'

'That's not what I heard from Jean.'

'How do you mean?'

I felt the graze of her scorn. 'You don't know very much, do you? Ask Georges yourself. What's the point of brains if you can't crack eggs? Take my word for it. Fancy-boy Georges and Jean have got their eyes on something. Don't know what. Don't care a bugger, either, as long as I get my share. They can go piss themselves, those two. *Des pompiers, tous les deux.*'

'Firemen?'

'*Pipe, pompier, tu sais.*' She pumped her fist up and down. 'Those two – what a drag. Right now, I'm going out. A little turn to see what's on. Want to come too?'

'Some other time, maybe. There are things I should do, work, classes. I'm expected at the university.'

'Suit yourself,' said Sylvie, looking bored. 'Sounds pretty dull to me.'

After the front door had slammed shut for the third time that morning I dressed and went out, stopping off at a seedy bar where I ate a quick croissant, hiding behind a pillar in case Sylvie dropped by, changing tables when the man nearest to me lit up a huge fat *mais* cigarette that choked me with its pall of burnt rags.

I waited so long for the bus I lost heart and returned to the now silent villa, determined to establish my presence there so that Georges wouldn't (didn't) recognise the room when he came back late that night with an armful of lilies, some of which I gave to Sylvie – lilies already several days past their best but in the dark, you couldn't tell.

Only their smell, that's what I remember, the smell that now invades this room as I sit waiting for Kate, that settles like dust among the family photographs in their silver frames, Stephen and I on our wedding day, open-faced smiles, Stephen's bushy fair hair already peaked at the crown; the photographs that should have been of children but aren't because we don't have any though not for want of trying. The children who might plug the void at the centre of our shared lives, whose absence we never mention in a Wittgensteinian way (you know the bit I mean: whereof we cannot speak we must pass over in silence). I wish it hadn't happened like this. I wish there was *something* we could do – I could do – to make up for what happened so long ago.

Who knows precisely how cause is linked to effect? Maybe the problem lay elsewhere. Maybe it wasn't my fault. I wish . . . Never mind. There's the swish of Kate's car in the drive, the crunch of well-tended gravel and Sam's enthusiastic *halloos*. Wishing is for kids, anyway.

ELEVEN

All the time we lived in the villa, a little under a month, I rarely spent time alone with Jean. Sylvie saw to that. The instant she heard the crashing of the front door, which he opened with a well-placed kick to the frame, she would shoot out of her room and start yelling straight away. Her abuse ricocheted ineffectually off his broad back. One day she came to my room with a black eye and purple bruising down the side of her face. It wasn't Jean, she said sullenly (I hadn't asked), but neither did she volunteer any more positive information.

Sometimes the four of us ate together in our room when Georges came home at night, picnicking on whatever he could salvage from Carrefour: overripe tomatoes, damaged fruit and offcuts from the *charcuterie* no prudent customer would buy. Even Sylvie was impressed by the room's transformation. To make it feel more like home I had pinned some posters to the wall, a couple of early Bob Dylans and a psychedelic moon. Sylvie said she liked the watery moon but the git with the guitar gave her the creeps.

The crates came and went. They must have been moved during the day when I went to class and though I felt uneasy at the thought of someone messing about in my absence (Jean? Sylvie? an unknown accomplice?) there didn't seem much point in making a fuss. The others were doing us a favour: who was I to complain?

Only once was I bold enough to pry, returning earlier than usual to an empty house that was eerily still. A new crate had appeared in the room, smaller than the rest. Thinking it might serve as a bedside table, I started to shift it myself when I noticed the uppermost boards were loose. It didn't take long to get inside.

Packed in straw I found a plaster bust of Napoleon. I'm not sure what I was expecting – certainly not this. Despite a chipped nose he brought to the squalor of our surroundings a certain imperial class. With some apprehension at what the others might say I shoved the straw back in the crate, put Boney on top and pushed him into a corner. He looked a little forlorn so I hacked down some ivy in the yard, knotting its leaves into a victory crown. A rakish angle suited him best.

Merde à Dieu was Georges's immediate reaction on finding himself face to face with the Emperor. '*T'es royaliste, ou quoi?*'

'No. I like him, that's all. I found him in one of the crates.'

'Ah *non*, Janey. This is too much. I'm not going to have that old scumbag keeping watch in a corner. Put him back.'

'Don't be silly. I like him.'

'*Dingue*, that's what you are. He was an *emmerdeur* like all the rest.'

'Not at first. In the early days he was fine.'

'Beginnings are not important. What counts is the end. We can all dance the tango, in the beginning. But later – things turn out badly, you'll see.'

We compromised by twisting his face to the wall where he remained for several days until the ivy began to droop. Then Boney and his box disappeared. I assumed Georges had ordered his summary removal and thought nothing more about it.

After the first few days I went back to class, determined to make amends for my recent inattention. Anyway, I missed Kate and with Georges out at Carrefour all day I had very little to do. Kate noticed a change in me. She said I had become very snappy: was anything wrong? I tried to tell her about the house but she thought I was exaggerating. She says I often do.

'How's Georges, anyway?'

'He's fine. But he works all the time. He says we'll go away soon, somewhere south. Provence, Monte Carlo.'

'You don't seem too pleased.'

'I am really. It's just that, well, I don't see much of him. Maybe later, things will improve.'

I was marking time. It wasn't that I had stopped loving the man – I still went funny whenever he walked into the room – but I felt my own familiar self slipping away. Without Georges I was nothing and as he was out all day and much of the night I became less and less substantial to the point where I wondered if I existed at all. Unnerved to find myself the figment of another's imagination I did my best to etch a solid pattern to my life, leaving the house soon after Georges, breakfast at the student canteen, classes, lunch with Kate, more classes, library, quick sunbathe on the grass if the weather was fine, back inside when skies were dull, bus home at 6 p.m. where I would scuttle to my room, attempt some desultory cleaning then settle down on the mattress to read, moving to the window when the light began to fade and if it went completely before Georges's return I would stare at darkening cracks in the concrete outside.

★   ★   ★

Clever Mr Jones, volunteering an opinion on Robbe-Grillet's *Dans le labyrinthe*, suggested that the author's dehumanising technique of tracing patterns in the snow, up sundry wallpapers, across dust-ridden surfaces in some anonymous room (that might or might not have been a picture on the wall) added little to our experience of the human condition. 'That's a personal opinion,' he added. 'I don't think it tells us very much.'

'It says a lot about wallpaper,' I protested, which raised an unintended titter.

Afterwards, the professor in charge of our group said he was pleased I had begun to take my studies seriously. If I continued down the same path, I might even do well.

Every few days Kate passed on a letter from my parents who continued to bombard me with questions about Georges, most of which I ignored. Kate wondered why I withheld my new address. I said I wasn't sure but somehow I couldn't bring myself to tell them about my latest move, not even with the usual embellishments with which I disguised the truth.

> I'm fine, really. Sorry I haven't written for ages but I've started to work hard. I've got this essay to write on French philosophy. Descartes drives me round the bend. He maintains that the reason why we have the idea of perfection is because God gives it to us. If God is the ultimate of perfection he must exist because existence is more perfect than non-existence. That seems daft to me. Though I don't believe you can 'prove' the existence of God one way or the other he could surely have come up with a more robust argument than that. And how do I know the thinking 'I' exists when nobody would ever call *me* perfect?
>
> You say I hardly mentioned Georges in my last letter. No, we haven't fallen out. He's very busy at work so I'm

not seeing as much of him as I'd like. Otherwise, everything's fine. They're doing a stock inventory after the store closes and there's talk of sending him on a management course, so promotion is definitely on the cards.

His mother took us out again last weekend, to the same inn by the river Garonne which I told you about. This time wasn't quite so successful. I was feeling really tired, Georges was too, and the ghastly *patron* persuaded Madame Delvaux to sing for everyone. As we were outside, there wasn't even a piano. I thought she was bound to refuse but no, she only had to be asked a couple of times before she leapt to her feet and launched into some aria, Puccini, she told us later. Everyone stopped eating and stared at the three of us, with the *patron* fluttering about in the background having rapturous heart-attacks. I don't think I've ever been so embarrassed in my life. Georges and I didn't dare look at each other in case we started to giggle.

Afterwards, she sat down beaming at the applause, which seemed genuine enough, and asked if I wanted to follow her example. Imagine! I told her I couldn't sing to save my life. Madame disagreed, saying everyone could sing if they only put their minds to it. I said it wasn't my mind that was the problem and I could tell, from the look she gave me, that she thought I was being rude. On the way back, the radiator cracked and we had to wait for ages for the mechanic to arrive. By the time we got her back to Bordeaux she had missed her favourite telly programme and I'm sure she blamed it all on me. Or am I just getting paranoid? That's what love does, I suppose.

Sorry – I'm in a bad mood, don't mind me. Sometimes I wonder if I'm doing the right thing then I know that everything will fall into place when I come home for my final year. All is for the best in the best of all possible worlds. Some of the philosophy rubs off so it's maybe not wasted after all. I'll be more cheerful next time, I promise you.

We were always making promises, Georges and I. I'll marry you next year (sometime, never). I'll take you away from here, I promise, to the land beyond dreams. Tomorrow we'll go to the ocean, yes, we shall, but when tomorrow came he would have something else planned, some man he had to see, business, don't ask what, we'll go another day, so by the time we finally set out for the coast, one Sunday in July, I had almost given up the wanting. Things got bad, you see. They usually do.

The sun was already high when we crept out of the house, banging the front door behind us. In the hot dusty air I felt my spirits rise. Georges sparkled with boyish enthusiasm. I saw him only in the dark, the half-dark at best. He had become as shadowy as myself.

We took a wide sweep through the outskirts of the city, stopping off for a late breakfast in one of the cafés around the stadium.

Georges dropped his *tartine* into his coffee, a habit I found vaguely disgusting. He asked if I was happy. I said I wasn't sure but on balance, probably yes.

'*Les Anglais*,' he said, spooning out brownish lumps of bread, 'you talk like shopkeepers, all of you. *En balance, merde.*'

'I don't see why you lump us all together. You asked me a question. I try to answer as honestly as I can.'

'I'm not sure honesty is your strongest suit, *ma petite*.'

'I'm honest with you. The others – I don't give a damn about them.'

'And with yourself?'

'Of course.' I answered without hesitation. Without thinking, either.

'You worry me, sometimes, Janey. Behind that mask of yours, you might be happy, you might be sad. Who am I to tell?'

I said, 'Look at me now.'

He raised his eyes. I saw a man in his mid-thirties, a man with an elfin slant to his eyes, leathery skin, pointed nose like a ferret's, a man you could trust with your heart though probably not your purse. A *gueule de tête*, as they say.

'What do you see?' I asked, leaning forward across the table.

'I see myself in your eyes, two eyes, one nose, a pair of lips, a thousand, million hairs, can't count properly – *j'ai raté mon bachot, tu vois* – the face of a young girl, a young woman who has said she will marry me but . . .'

'No buts. I said I would, later. You know why I can't just yet.'

'I know what you tell me. That may not be quite what you mean.'

I refused to take this seriously. What I told Georges was the truth, the whole truth and nothing but the truth. What I told myself was my business.

Downstairs in the WC, I stared at my reflection in the blistered mirror next to the broom cupboard. Two greyish-blue eyes, a nose I never liked, dark fringe, cracked lips, oatmeal skin. It didn't look like me.

At the door I turned to look again.

My face wasn't there.

There was, I know, a logical explanation: one of the hooks had pulled loose so the mirror was angled away from the door. My face wasn't there because the angle was wrong. Nothing personal.

Back in the café I noticed a couple of youths playing the pinball machines near our table. Georges had his back to them. They saw me and went over to the far side of the

111

room. Bikers, I assumed from their black leathers. Shifty types. You saw a lot of them round here.

Georges paid (I had to lend him the money) then we went outside.

The leather seats had scorched in the sun. I suggested we buy a picnic. Georges said no: we would find somewhere to eat by the ocean. As I would have to pay I wasn't too happy with this: it would have to be something cheap.

I had forgotten the youths from the café when we stopped at some lights and heard a hooting from the car next to ours. One of the youths was hanging out of the window, gesticulating at Georges. The other made yodelling noises as he hunched over the wheel.

'Are they friends of yours?' I asked.

'Never seen them before.'

'What do they want?'

'You'll see.'

When the lights turned green Georges advanced in the outside lane. The other car stayed abreast. Once or twice the driver shot out his hand and banged on our car. Despite the heat I quickly closed my window.

At the open road Georges put his foot down hard. I was jerked backwards into my seat. He pointed to the safety handle above the door. 'You might need that,' he said. 'Things will likely get rough.'

It was the first time we had driven at speed. Real speed. I felt exhilarated, not scared. Georges thrust the Gordini into the lead. In the mirror, I watched the youths' thwarted attempts to pull out. Once they nearly clipped a passing car whose angry horn was quickly left behind. Trees on either side, poplars, vanishing to a point ahead. White trunks speeding past. A farm, a hamlet, then a whole village passed in a blur.

I opened the window.

The smell of pines hit me in the face. I started to laugh. Any sound was drowned in the roar of the engine, the thundering of tyres on tarmac.

We entered the forest. The other car had now inched into the centre of the road.

'Shut it,' said Georges, nodding at the window.

I did as he asked.

Georges looked steely-calm. Eyes front. Sometimes he glanced up at the mirror. The car behind wove in and out. Georges kept to the centre of the road, blocking their attempts to overtake. I saw they were creeping up the inside. Georges swore. '*Elle est foutue, cette bagnole.*' Theirs or ours? Couldn't tell. At the bend, they dropped back. A lorry hurtled past on the other side. The needle had reached 150,160,170. I felt the first flash of fear. We hit a new stretch of road, wide and straight. Cuttings on either side, a green mass of trees, fuzzy from speed.

Again, the other car pushed its way up the inside. The side next to me. I turned to see the driver, head bent over the wheel, teeth bared like a wolfhound. The second man leant over the seats, his body arched by the car's velocity. He raised his arm. Did I really see what happened next? Or is it what I thought I saw? Speed alters perception. Makes you see what isn't there. Makes you blind to what is.

The man had a gun in his hand. The gun pointed at me.

I screamed.

Georges said, 'Hold tight.' And then, ignoring my scream, he turned the wheel to the right. Just a fraction.

We skidded across the path of the other car. My side would take the impact. The car with a gun-toting maniac. A gun pointing at me. I clung with all my strength to the

113

handle. There was a loud clunk. Georges struggled with the wheel. The other car wasn't there any more. I felt myself thrown against the door. The door held. We were sliding across the road. If anything came now, *foutu*. *Between grief and nothing, I will take grief.* But I wanted – desperately – to live.

A car rounded the bend. It bore down on us, fast.

I said a prayer for the living and the dead. Shut my eyes tight. Georges would call me a coward. He diced with my life.

You *idiot*.

Then Georges came out of the skid. We shot in front of the oncoming car. I saw the driver's terrified face. Turned round as he pulled over to the verge.

The car with the two youths had disappeared. They must have left the road. Clouds of dust from a long way back. We squealed round the bend. Couldn't see any more. We should go back and check. Maybe they needed help.

Not bad, that one, not bad at all. But . . . But what? You'll see. They're all the same, really. Cinglés, dingues. Des salopards, vraiment.

Georges kept his eyes on the road, arms braced on the wheel. My knuckles on the safety strap. The lumpy whiteness of bone beneath the skin. I forced myself to breathe, in one two, out one two, in one two, chest clanking like a bilge pump.

After several miles he reached for my hand. To go back was stupid. One of them had a gun. If they saw us clambering down the embankment they might blow our heads off.

Hard earth at my back. I feel a rock at the base of my spine. Star-shaped light in the trees. A foulness of rotting matter, fungal, of life feeding off death. My open knees on the forest floor forming a wide letter 'V'.

This man: my wanting him isn't a game. We collide like immutable objects. One moves, the other doesn't. That's anger for you. Anger tempered with the alloy of my love. His love. Our love. If you chanced upon us in the forest you would surely see sparks fly.

TWELVE

I never felt the same about Stephen, let's be honest about
that. From the day of our wedding I had a clear idea
of how our lives would evolve and I wasn't far wrong:
ours was, I have to say, an entirely rational affair. We
were married in June under unseasonally grey skies that
brightened suddenly as we posed on the church steps,
turning my official smiles into a scowl. Kate said I looked
radiant: I think she was just being kind. At least Stephen
behaved well, talking dahlias to Auntie Bets and cricket
to Dad while my brother got publicly drunk for the first
time and made Mum cry.

As for life at home, you shift with the tide, you see
your friends get married one by one, see the lives they
lead, see the helpless, squally children they produce and
you think: I'd like that too, why not, so you go through
the motions like everyone else. And if you sometimes
wonder whether you haven't missed something out of
the equation, something terribly, utterly important, you
don't know what it is and most of the time you don't stop
to think. What's the point of brains if you can't crack eggs?
That's what Sylvie used to say and her 'philosophy' was
just as serviceable as mine.

I shouldn't complain. The fact that we are childless is
no fault of Stephen's. The doctors blamed my plumbing,

an infection that had blocked off the tubes. There were things we could try, however slim our chances of success. Stephen, who wanted children as much as I did, entrusted the decision to me. I went into hospital for an exploratory operation that left me feeling for days afterwards as if someone had stirred my insides with a long-handled spoon and though I could have continued with further operations, I decided to leave it to fate who dealt me her usual hand.

Questioned about the probable date of my infection, the doctors gave their qualified opinion that it was relatively well established. In their terms that meant anything between two and ten years. I counted back and reached a date of 1972. I'm glad they stopped then. If it had been any earlier I might have blamed the infection on Georges and I'm not sure I could have borne the strain of knowing that Stephen suffers because of something I did with Georges. Because I opened my legs for him, don't be coy. Because I knew the risks yet failed to take the necessary precautions. No, I couldn't bear that.

I'm not particularly good with children; does that make it any easier? A class of schoolkids, fine, I have learned how to exercise control but a child on its own puts me on my guard. Sometimes I watch Kate with the boys and know I haven't the mettle for it. While they were staying with me, Sam took me out into the garden and asked how long it would take him to dig a hole to the centre of the earth. I told him I didn't know exactly and anyway, the question was irrelevant. Stephen wouldn't let him anywhere near the flowerbeds and he would frazzle to death before he reached the earth's core.

How far down? he wanted to know. A hundred yards, a mile, two miles, I said I didn't know exactly. It gets hotter as you go down and he'd run out of drilling machinery.

117

'Just suppose,' he said stubbornly, frowning at my feet, 'I didn't run out of machinery. And just suppose I didn't frazzle to death, then how long would it take?'

'One week,' I said firmly.

He thought about this for a moment, then shook his head. 'I think it would take *years.*'

'You may well be right. It depends, doesn't it?

'Depends on what?'

'I don't know. How hard you stick at it. Whether you work all night and all day. How good your equipment is. How many men you use.'

'What if you use women?'

'Women too. Lots of things.'

He started fiddling with his shirt. 'You don't know the answer, do you?' I thought he was going to cry.

'No, Sam, I don't. To be honest, it's not something I've thought much about.'

'Well, I think about it all the time. I'm going to ask Mum, she'll know.'

'Why does it matter?'

He stared at me scornfully as if I had asked the dumbest question in the world. Children often do this with me. 'Because I've started digging a hole in my garden back home, that's why. I need to know how long it will take.'

'To reach the centre of the earth?'

He nodded.

'But, Sam, that's impossible.'

'Mum says if I keep trying I'll get there in the end.'

I started to tell him that was nonsense, he'd never make it, then I thought: no, Kate's right, it's better to dream than to submit to the obstacles of practical men who will tell you why you can't and never how you can. Who knows? He might even strike lucky. I heard him pestering Kate in the

118

kitchen. She wasn't able to answer his question any more than I had but she managed along the way to impart some simple principles of arithmetic. *If you dig twenty feet in a day, how many feet will you dig in seven days? No, Sam, not twenty-seven, seven* times *twenty, which is how much? One hundred and forty, that's right, Sam, very good. Seven days make one week and how many weeks in a year? We'll need your calculator for this next bit . . .*

Kate stopped me before I went to bed, saying I looked unusually tired: had I thought of taking a holiday? I surely had several weeks over the summer when I could get right away. I should count myself lucky, she said. She always found the summer holidays a pain. Had I thought what I might do?

I told her I wasn't sure.

'Can Stephen take you anywhere?'

'Too busy, he says. I might go somewhere on my own.'

'Any idea where?'

I said, 'France.'

She said, 'Why France?'

I said, 'Why on earth not? It's as good a place as anywhere else.'

THIRTEEN

The night before our enforced departure from the villa Georges and Jean came home together very late laden with hampers of food: pâté, caviar, *foie gras*, olives from Tuscany, salami from Milan, bread, apricots, salads, tomatoes, champagne (the best) and two bottles of Beaumes de Venise. Jean had also brought flowers for Sylvie, real ones, not cast-offs from Carrefour. Sylvie asked what the fuck he thought he was doing: no one had bloody died. He said they'd cost him a packet, she could fucking well show some appreciation for a change or he'd take them home to his wife. Irène would find a way of showing gratitude, that's for sure.

Sylvie left the flowers lying in the hall where Georges trod on them accidentally so she stuck them any-old-how into an empty jar. Despite her affected indifference, I could tell she was pleased.

Leaving the men to drink their beers in the yard Sylvie and I prepared my room for the feast, making tables from empty packaging and lighting all the candles we could find. She put the flowers in Boney's empty corner then disappeared to change. As a final touch I draped a cotton shawl over the window and nearly set the house alight when it singed in the flames.

Sylvie wiggled back wearing a spangly dress that was

about as decent as a stripper's pouch. Not to be outdone I kept the others waiting while I searched my bags for something *outré* to match her mood. The best I could manage was a strip of faded batik worn native-style over a swimsuit, psychedelic pink, with matching hoops at my ears.

Georges laughed when he saw me, saying I looked good enough to eat. I said we had better things on the menu: the food tasted divine.

Georges, Sylvie and I sat on the mattress, Jean on the floor closest to the champagne which meant he helped himself more than we did yet he remained obstinately sober in contrast to Sylvie who wormed her way to sit between Georges and me, rubbing against his back and giggling at the stories he told about his colleagues at Carrefour.

Bertrand had fallen hopelessly in love with one of the check-out girls, daughter of *pieds-noirs*, with breasts like ripe melons. Georges made a gesture with his hands. The girl was engaged to someone else, a boy she didn't love, and toyed with poor Bertrand's affections until he was driven wild with desire. Bertrand swore that if she kept her legs shut much longer he would buy himself a gun. 'That one,' I said, 'he wouldn't hurt a fly.'

'Who cares about flies?' asked Sylvie. 'If he's got half the balls you say he has, just send him round to me.'

The candles died one by one. Our shadows became more pronounced. Jean's ran the height of one wall then bent back over the ceiling. I pointed this out to Sylvie. 'So what?' she said. 'He promises a fucking cucumber and all you get is a measly courgette.' Jean, leaning his weight on a crate, shrugged and smiled to himself: he didn't seem to care.

Georges said the manager had been seen in his office by one of the caretakers, his hand down a supervisor's blouse. The union bosses were trying to persuade the woman to lodge a formal complaint. She insisted it was all quite innocent. 'More flies, I suppose, or was it ants, this time?' sniggered Sylvie.

A distant hum of traffic on the highway. The room had started to spin – nothing I couldn't control but when Jean next passed me the bottle I pushed it away.

Georges went out, taking a candle with him.

After a time, Sylvie picked herself up from the mattress, said she had to pee and wobbled out of the door.

Jean and I were left alone.

Jean said, 'So that's how it is.'

I said, 'No, it isn't like that at all. Sylvie, she doesn't mean any harm.'

'You think?' He called me *vous*. I wasn't sure if that was normal with Jean. We encountered each other so rarely I couldn't remember a previous conversation. His face in shadow looked repellently ugly. I couldn't help staring at his nose.

I said, 'Thinking doesn't come in to it. I know.'

He said, 'You think you're smart, don't you? All those *bouquins* – can't see the point of them, myself.'

We glared at each other in the dark. People don't usually take against me. I am neither bold enough nor significant enough to attract strong feelings either way. I am merely Janey, Crazy Jane. *Wants to be a painter, does she? Couldn't paint her toe-nails if she tried.* 'Sylvie really likes you,' I said dumbly. He made no effort to conceal his contempt.

Georges and Sylvie returned carrying between them an old record player and a stack of LPs – Johnny Halliday, Barbara, some early Rolling Stones, Serge Reggiani. She wanted to dance, she said, dance until she dropped.

Georges held me tight as we shuffled round the crates. I could feel myself swaying precariously whenever he loosened his grip. By Sylvie's flowers he pushed me against the wall, forcing my legs apart with his knee. My skirt got in the way. Over Georges's shoulder I watched the other two. Jean had planted himself in the centre of the room while Sylvie sashayed back and forth, wiggling her bottom and making snake-like movements with her tongue.

Who was it that suggested we change partners? It might have been Sylvie but I think, honestly, the blame rests with me. Georges wasn't keen. I remember saying I wanted to experience a giant waltz, *une valse géante* (no one laughed) but really I wanted to make Jean like me and dancing was the only way I knew.

Sylvie switched records. To a lisping Françoise Hardy she and Georges tried a jitterbug first but soon gave up to paddle around the floor. Sylvie's matchstick heels meant she had to hook her neck over his shoulder as she attempted to snuggle close.

Jean's idea of dancing was to shift his weight from one foot to the other without giving an inch. It was like dancing with the Eiger. I soon got the hang of it and drooped from his arms. As his bulk stood between me and the others I lost sight of what they were doing, lulled by Jean's insistent heartbeat that pulsed more strongly as Hardy skipped from one sentimental ballad to the next, aware of the thing between his legs that showed the first signs of life, the worm that turns into a nascent snake. What I might do with it formed no part of my plan. I simply wanted him to know I wasn't as bookish as he thought. I could play Sylvie's game if that's how they did things round here.

We reached the final fade. The stylus made scratching sounds as the record went round and round. Jean continued to sway from side to side, eyes closed, swollen dick pressed against my belly. His face seemed one mile high.

I hoped someone else would attend to the turntable. When no one did, I peered round his waist, looking for Georges. He wasn't there. Nor was Sylvie. I heard them next door, Georges and Sylvie, the man I meant to marry and his fishwife whore. Something banged against the wall. Now you hear them, now you don't. All cats are grey in the night, that's what my mother used to say. I wondered what she meant. I seem to have spent a good part of my life among people whose pointed asides never made the right connection.

Sylvie and Georges. Beauty and the Beast. Which is beauty, for God's sake? Sylvie might have been OK, once, until she was rollered so many times you could see the tramlines leading to her cunt. The cunt that Georges, even now . . . That one stuck his prick in places you wouldn't trust your umbrella. Any old port in a storm. In out. Rain or shine. That's how I got infected. Stands to reason, doesn't it? Play with fire and sooner or later you'll get your fingers burnt. Or your prick.

Jean pushed me away with a gesture of disgust. 'Fuck this,' he said and stormed next door.

It was the first and only only time I heard him strike first. He hit her several times. She screamed at him to stop. Georges intervened. Jean might have hit him too, I don't know. I had buried my head in the blankets trying to blunt the edge of their insane anger.

An eruption of screams and yells followed by sickening thuds. Jean and Sylvie were fighting in the hall. One of them kicked open my door which juddered against the wall. Sylvie clawed at his face. The girl was half his size, and drunk. She kept falling down, pummelling his legs then rising to attack his chest, his head, tearing out fistfuls of hair.

He held her by the neck. She swivelled on the floor, trying to kick herself free. I ran to the other side of the room, whipping the shawl from the window. My bare foot struck something squishy. I was shaking all over. Through the open door I saw him raise one fist above her head as if he wanted to smash her skull.

'Georges,' I screamed, 'do something, for Christ's sake. He'll kill her.'

The big man lifted his head. His eyes focused with difficulty. When he saw me he lumbered towards the door, dragging Sylvie by the neck. I thought he was coming for me. To stop myself crying out I stuffed the shawl in my mouth. Then he looked down. A moment's hesitation. Something snapped inside. Whatever else he had done to Sylvie he hadn't hit her before. Not hard. In lust, perhaps, not this. Releasing her neck, he covered his face with his hands, moaning like an idiot. Sylvie continued to kick and scream on the floor, arms locked around his knees. Every time she pulled herself up she fell down again. When she succeeded at last, steadying herself against the doorpost, she kicked him straight in the balls. The force sent her shoe spinning down the hall.

He jack-knifed in a scream of pain. She jumped on his back as he fell. The two of them rolled on the floor, Jean's head sticking through my door. Sylvie, kicking and yelling, tried to jam it shut. I squirmed at the crunch. The two had rolled away from the door. The rest I couldn't see. Georges had come into the hall. I think he held her legs, allowing Jean to stagger free. Jean stumbled towards the door, clutching

125

his pants and butting against the walls which rattled to the point of collapse.

Flinging open the door to the street, he shouted at Sylvie, 'You fucking lousy whore. That's the last time. Don't expect to see me again. Couldn't blow up a balloon, that's your fucking problem. Not one lousy balloon. Take your stinking *cul* down to the docks and *vas te faire foutre*. That's all you're good for.'

The front door slammed.

Georges held on to Sylvie as long as he could. She bit and scratched and finally kicked herself free. Her screams got fainter as she chased Jean down the darkened street, chased him in her spangly dress and one stiletto shoe. Cunts and pricks: words I understood but not the things she did with them, the things she swore she would do to him and to his lilywhite wife, if she ever caught up with the bitch.

For a time, I felt too paralysed to move. The house was deathly still. A faint scratching from the hall. Georges, perhaps, I hadn't heard him leave. But I couldn't bear to face him, not after what he'd done with Sylvie, what I'd nearly done with Jean. Cunts and pricks. Same old story. Same old bloody carousel. And when the music stops, change your partners for the dance, hurry, now, please, can't keep the others waiting, in out, up down, turn yourself around. All cats are grey in the night. Same with cunts. No big deal. Try it yourself, one day. Stick your head in a paper bag and see if it makes the blindest bit of difference, to anyone.

I went to bed fully clothed, lying stiffly against the wall. When Georges entered the room, I felt my breath turn slow.

'*Génie*,' he said, very softly, '*tu dors déjà?*'

Breathe through the nose, one, two, three, four, five, hold it, one, two, out, three, four, five.

I sensed him climbing in next to me, in, one, two, three, four, five, out, one, two, three, four, five. His hand on my thigh. I wanted desperately to push it away, rub the spot where he had touched my flesh, but I couldn't, could I? I was meant to be asleep so I willed myself to believe that my thigh belonged to someone else, anyone, it didn't matter to whom, as long as it wasn't me he touched, me he stroked and caressed in this filthy stinking house, while I lay helpless as a baby, flat on my back and fast asleep, but if he tried anything else I'd stick him in the throat, sure as God I would.

Loud banging at the door. Georges ran into the room. I opened my eyes. My head hurt like hell. I thought he was still in bed, next to me. The room was filled with light. Bright light. Couldn't think straight. Plates and bottles everywhere. Sylvie's flowers scattered like reeds across the floor. A bright red shawl lay beside me on the bed. I'd snatched it down from the window the night before to muffle their screams. That much I remembered. The smell of food made me gag.

Georges was running about the room, stuffing clothes into a suitcase. My clothes. Bob Dylan shot off the wall, followed by the spangled moon which gave a loud rip as it came away in his hands. He shoved them into the suitcase, looking round for more.

'What the hell d'you think you're doing?'

'Get up.'

'Answer me.'

'Don't argue. Just do as I fucking say.'

'You're off your head.'

'So will you be if you don't come quick.'

He pulled me out of bed. I was wearing my clothes from the night before. The swimsuit and the piece of cloth. He said, 'Jesus Christ. How do you propose to explain that?'

'You're the one who needs to explain.'

He passed me a sweater and a skirt. 'These'll do,' he said. 'Get dressed.'

'I am dressed. Do for what? Georges, what's going on?'

'We have less than a minute to clear out.'

Foutre le camp, was what he said. Fuck the whole bloody camp. Still mad at him, I hopped off the bed and started pulling on the skirt over my swimsuit. He said I should take it off then decided we hadn't time.

'Time for what? Georges, you've got to tell me what's going on.'

'*Les flics*. That bitch last night, someone grassed. Said we were running a brothel. They'll be here any minute. Can't you hurry up, for God's sake?'

The news threw me into a panic. I couldn't fasten the zip. Georges had to do it for me. My hands had started to shake. I held on to his shoulders while he fiddled at my waist.

'How do you know?'

'A friend at the station. He called me at work. Don't worry about that.' He thrust my arms into the sweater. 'OK. Let's go.'

'Where, Georges? Where can we go?'

He passed me some bags and both of us ran for the door.

Half-way down the steps I remembered a book I had left in Sylvie's room. A grammar book. She'd asked to borrow it, God knows why.

'Don't be a fool,' said Georges. 'You can't go back in there.'

'It's got my name in it. If they find it, they might come looking.'

'They won't know where you are.'

128

'The name of the university – it's written next to mine. And the date. I always do that.'

'Too bad,' he said, looking grim. I had no choice but to follow him down the steps.

The Gordini was parked several blocks away. I couldn't open the front door, still buckled after the chase. Georges kept promising to get it fixed at his uncle's garage but always found excuses to delay. He opened the back for me and I slid with my case on to the seat, keeping my head down. Georges waited until the police van came screaming round the corner then pulled out carefully and drove away.

We went to his mother's who had gone to visit her family at Limoges. She stayed away for several days. Georges said we were quite safe as long as I didn't show my face. The neighbours might see: after the villa fiasco, we couldn't take any chances. Because of the grammar book I daren't return to the university and so would miss the end–of–term tests. I hoped they weren't important.

More seriously, our change in circumstance meant I couldn't see Kate. I needed to warn her about the grammar book and so, fortified by a tumbler of Madame Delvaux's Madeira, I telephoned the Gilberts who treated me with obvious disdain. Kate was out (or so they said). I asked if they could pass on a message. My mother had been taken ill. I had to return home unexpectedly and could they ask Kate to tell my tutor? I'd write to him myself, straight away, before leaving France.

'I hope it is nothing serious,' said Monsieur Gilbert. Voice like broken glass.

'No, not at all. Well, I mean, yes it is, otherwise I wouldn't need to go home. But I'm hoping it won't be . . . you know . . .'

'We hope so, too, for your poor mother's sake. And you will miss your examinations. Tzut. Tzut. They will not be pleased. Well, *bong chance.*'

'*Vous aussi, Monsieur.*'

I felt like spitting when I put down the phone. I wrote to my tutor, explaining about my mother's illness, and scribbled a further note to Kate saying that if the police came looking for me she wasn't to worry on my account but could she tell them that several of my books had been stolen from the student canteen, including an advanced grammar book? It was important she told them that. I hadn't reported the theft because only my books went missing – no money or possessions of value. I'd write again as soon as I could. *Grosses bises*, etc.

The rest of the time I paced that tiny, airless apartment, poking my finger into the cages of Madame Delvaux's fourteen canaries whose constant tweeting got on my nerves. I was tempted to open the doors and let them fly away. Then I grew fond of them, gave them all names – Pepée, Cocotte, Nana, Ma Biche, Mon Jules, the names that Georges had given me, pleased to distinguish one from the other. Pigeons came to the window, tapping their beaks against the glass. I didn't dare open. Someone might see.

Once I heard a soft rapping at the door, a querulous woman's voice through the keyhole. '*Vous êtes là, Madame Delvaux?*' My heart went stiff. She must have heard my caged footsteps walking from the window to the wall, up and down, till I thought I'd go mad.

When the voice at last gave up and feet shuffled back along the hall I crept into Georges's room which opened directly off his mother's. Smaller than a box room, its one high-up window looked on to the sooty well of the apartment block. Heavy rosewood bed. Mismatched wardrobe used as a coat

130

stand, his clothes draped on the outside. An open chest packed with plastic bags full of engine parts and odd shoes, nothing of interest to me.

The only clue to the occupant's identity was a yellowing photograph tucked into the mirror.

The woman had shoulder-length auburn hair, a girlishly pretty face – if you liked them that way – and long, shapely legs. I thought she was dead. Maybe that explained her presence here. She was bending over a boy of about four or five, his son Pascal, I suppose. The child's face was unformed: any family resemblance was indistinct.

Mother and son looked up towards the camera, both on the edge of laughter. You can play at happiness until your face turns blue, till words and gestures flow like a well-rehearsed script but you can't feign the real thing. Maybe Georges was not the one holding the camera. Maybe they laughed for someone else. Maybe, maybe. To hell with that. These two had a carefree innocence that made them both glow. What did I have? What could I possibly offer to compensate for their loss? Georges swore on his life that he loved me. I was no longer sure what that meant for either of us.

Feeling dead inside I hunted for some reminder of me that Georges treasured enough to display in his room, something that made *him* smile as he thought of me. My sketch of Georges in his car, Sacred Monsters, I had given it to him by the ocean. I couldn't find it though I searched all afternoon. The bare facts of my existence did not appear to have carried over into this poky little room where he slept in close proximity to his mother when he wasn't sleeping with me.

That night Georges was unbearably gentle. We couldn't go on like this. He said we should go away, we'd talked about it often enough. Now was the time. He would leave his work and together we'd head north.

'I thought we were going south,' I said petulantly.

North, south, what did it matter as long as we stayed together? As long as we went to a place far away where we could start afresh? Fresh as a daisy and a bloom in May. Bordeaux stinks, he said. Whispered, actually. Because of old Big-ears we couldn't even talk to each other without being shit-scared that someone might give us away, to his mother or to the *flics*. Either way we'd be fucked.

FOURTEEN

La Colombe
Vienne

Dear Mum and Dad

You'll see from the address that I've moved away from Bordeaux. Georges was owed a lot of holiday and when he goes back they've promised to promote him to Manager. The last one got the sack just before we left. So we're here for the next month at least. The place belongs to an uncle, a cousin, I'm not sure – very primitive, I can tell you. With only one tap (cold, of course) Georges has had to rig up a shower in the garden next to the front door, attaching a length of hose to the sprinkler from a watering can. The lavatory is round the side in one of the outhouses, surprisingly clean. It isn't even a water closet, just a wooden box with its own lavatory seat placed over a deep black pit in the ground. Every two days you throw yoghurt down the hole and hope for the best. The yoghurt has to be live, apparently, or else it won't work.

I love it here. The fields around are full of sunflowers, they're huge, taller than me, and everything scorched by the sun. It feels hotter than Bordeaux though we're some way north. The closest town is La Roche-Posay, with its Romanesque church, its square, a supermarket we rarely use as we get most of our food from the farm, chickens and tomatoes and jugs of milk. The farmer, Monsieur Caron, is over seventy: his four sons live in some of the other buildings and a daughter away in Châtellerault. This used to be a proper hamlet. Now there are only the Carons and us and a tax inspector who lives in the big house by the road and keeps very much to himself. We don't even know his name.

No one comes here, no tourists, I mean. The roads are empty; you wouldn't believe how lovely France can be when you escape the crowds. I feel happier than I have for weeks. Things were not going well – you must have guessed from the way my letters tailed off. Cities are foul in the summer, hot and dusty. Everyone gets horribly bad-tempered including Georges who was working so hard I hardly got to see him. Now we're together all the time. I know you won't approve but we won't have long before the summer ends. I miss the ocean, of course, and Kate who might come for a visit. When we last spoke, she wasn't sure about her plans.

There isn't a phone here, not even a payphone in the hamlet (I told you it was primitive) so write to me often. I wish you could see this place. There's something magic about it. In place of rent we've agreed to tend the garden which is more stones than anything else and choked with weeds. The work breaks your back but at the end of the day you see the freshly turned earth, see the heaps of discarded stones and you feel an absurd sense of pride that you can achieve so much (or so little) on your own.

I've also started work on my dissertation. I told you I was thinking of concentrating on the troubadour poets. Old French was my best paper in Part Is and it seemed crazy not to continue. That's had to change: there aren't any books here and the local library can't help so I've switched subjects and am now writing about Rimbaud. He's one of my favourite poets, one of the best that France has ever produced, a true visionary who believed he could create a new language, an alchemy of words in which he invented the colour of vowels and went through hell to find them. When he was nineteen he gave it all up, travelled to Aden and on to Abyssinia where he ran guns to King Menelek in the interior. I've got a book of his letters. *Maintenant je puis dire que l'art est une sottise.* Most of the time he moaned about how bored he was, endlessly exploited. Gold was what he wanted now, real gold, not the fool's gold of words. But everything went wrong.

His partner died. He was saddled with debts. Menelek, crafty sod, wouldn't pay and then Rimbaud fell sick and was forced to return home to France, broken and virtually penniless. They cut off his leg in Marseilles and he died soon afterwards, recounting his visions to his sister Isabelle, still dreaming of a triumphant return to Abyssinia. It's such a sad story – to want so much and to fail so spectacularly. I'm very excited about it.

Actually, it was Georges who suggested the idea. We were talking one night when I happened to mention that I couldn't understand how such a great poet like Rimbaud could renounce literature for the sordid profession of gun-running. Georges said it was obvious: words were bound to fail sooner or later. If Rimbaud saw in them the symbol of gold, he would naturally turn his mind to the real thing. Symbols are like that, he said. You always want more in the end. It's all there in the poems, everything that happened to him later. *I turned silences and nights into words. I made the whirling world stand still . . . Crying, I saw gold AND COULD NOT DRINK.* Excuse the translation, it sounds much better in French, but can you understand how excited I feel?

Georges sends his love – you know I do. I can't wait to see you again. I'm not sure when I'll be back. It all depends on Georges's job. We'll have to see how long they will give him: I won't stay on here alone, don't worry about that. I know it sounds a bit vague. I think they're planning to send him to another store which hasn't opened yet. Say hello to Martin from me. I hope he's managing to keep out of trouble without me. All my love, Janey.

The letter's evidence is irrefutable. I must have been happy at La Colombe. *A la lisière de la forêt*, at the edge of the forest, *les fleurs de rêve tintent, éclatent, éclairent.* Rimbaud – who else? *Les Illuminations.* A poem called '*Enfance*'. We acted like children too, playing at happiness in our gingerbread house on the edge of the forest, its turquoise shutters quaintly festooned with vines.

135

Because of what came later I had forgotten that extraordinary interlude, an intermezzo lasting several weeks, three perhaps, or four, in which we drew close again, shutting the door on the world outside which could go hang itself as far as we were concerned. Under an eternal sun our lives settled into a rhythm of work and snatched siestas, of sex with creaking bones. All that had soured our relations in Bordeaux – Sylvie, Big Jean, the villa, Georges's work at the supermarket, his mother and her fourteen canaries, my bad conscience at things undone – we shed them like dead skin, emerging into a butterfly dawn. To wake in our huge iron bed, to fling open the shutters and see the sun shine green through the vines, to know the world was good and that we had returned each to the other, a little shakily at first but getting stronger every day: that was what mattered. The rest might never have happened. I make no apology for the dullness of my description. The illusion of happiness is always mundane.

After an early breakfast I would carry out a cane table to the shade of a mulberry tree at the edge of our domaine where I would work at my dissertation until noon, reading and making notes, more often staring at burnished fields that rolled towards the horizon, fields of sunflowers and corn, the winding road marked by a zigzag of dusty trees. Georges would either sleep late or potter about the barns. Spartan lunch (prepared by me) then an afternoon's work in the garden, digging, planting, raking stones. By dusk our bodies ached so badly we could scarcely move. Georges would spray me with the hose, I'd do the same to him and then, fresh and clean, he'd sit drinking wine in the yard while I made supper, salads and omelettes most nights, a chicken for a Sunday treat. To bed when darkness fell.

For the first time in my life I lived for what the day would

136

bring, innocent of the past and of the future, too. We talked only when we felt like it. I can't remember any of those conversations: we probably discussed the merits of endives over celeriac, things like that.

There was always the problem of money. Despite the Carons' generosity we still needed cash from somewhere. My funds were exhausted as it had always been assumed I would return home at the end of my course. My colourful interpretation of Georges's prospects prevented me from writing to my parents, as did my angry pride. Georges was equally broke, having quit his job without collecting his last pay cheque. He was owed money by Jean, he said, enough to keep us several months. As soon as he judged it safe, he would send Jean our address. In the meantime, there were things he could do. *Bricolage* was the word he used.

And so he started to disappear for days at a time, taking the Gordini and returning with a trunkful of junk – paintings, books, prints, dusty ornaments, stamps, old postcards, the odd piece of furniture. He had turned into some kind of knocker, buying cheap and selling dear. I didn't like it but without money of my own there was little I could say or do.

The days became irksomely long. One afternoon I thought: to hell with this and read a novel instead. That night Georges was late home, having driven almost to Limoges and back and made only one purchase of note: a young ballerina in bronze, exquisitely worked, arms floating above her slender head. She weighed more than I thought and I was struck by her many contrasts, between fluidity and mass, between serenity and the dancing master's hateful rod, and by the metalled cast of her fragile ambitions.

'She's beautiful, truly. Where did you find her?'

'At a place called Les Sablons. The château is falling apart yet they have treasures like this. I met the chatelaine: a woman of eighty, ninety, you can't tell with *bidoche* like that.'

'You must have paid a fortune.'

Georges shrugged. 'I paid enough but not that much. Here, take it. She's for you, *la valseuse.*'

'For me? Why?'

'Because you like her almost as much as I like you.'

She soon found a home: on the mantel in the bedroom where I could see her the moment I woke. She's mine, I would think with a burst of pride, our only possession of value and he gives her to me. I used her as a primitive alarm clock. As soon as the first chink of sun had inched its way along the mantel, suffusing the dancer's head and shoulders with greeny-gold light, I knew it was time to rise and I would slip silently out of bed, savouring the shock of cold stone flags on bare feet, into the kitchen where I would open the door in a dramatic expansion of light, squatting in my nightdress on the steps as the sun tingled my skin.

Then one day I opened my eyes and she wasn't there any more. Like Napoleon in Bordeaux my little dancer had disappeared.

Dear Jane
We haven't heard from you for two weeks now. I thought I should tell you that your mother is beginning to worry, you know what she's like. Your earlier letter arrived safely and we're both glad that you sound so very happy in your new abode. I'm sure that's why you haven't written. However, mothers being mothers, could you dispatch a card straight away to let us know that all is well? Better still, perhaps you could arrange to telephone, reversing the charges if need be. We're going to Ireland later in the month, usual place, so please, please, get in touch before then.

Martin's O level results came through at the beginning of the week. Would you believe it, he's got a '1' in all subjects except geography, which he failed. I always thought geography was his best subject. He's taking it very well. Until he knew how well he'd done, there was talk of leaving school but that is out of the question now. One of the masters came round last night to discuss the possibility of Oxford. (Why not Cambridge, I'd like to know?) If he works really hard, they think he can do it. After some determined skirmishing he has agreed to come to Ireland with us, so we're all sad you won't be able to come too. Unless you change your mind, that is. Anyway, call or write as soon as you can, to put your mother's mind at rest.

I thought I should also let you know that a letter has arrived for you from the university. I haven't opened it – when you're next in touch, you can tell me what I should do with it.

Please send my best regards to Georges. Tell him I've started to brush up my French. Terribly rusty, but there you go. The Institute put me in touch with a young Frenchie who comes in once a week. Your mother calls her my popsy. I must say, she's jolly good.

Till soon, young lady. Best wishes to you both. Pa.

I didn't call but I sent a card express and a hurried note to Kate at the Gilberts'. To my parents I wrote:

Everything fine. Sorry I haven't been in touch. The garden takes it out of me and by the time it's dark, I'm aching all over and haven't the energy to do more than eat supper and crawl into bed. Great news about Martin – I knew he'd do it in the end. Very sad, but I'll not be able to join you in Ireland. Maybe soon after that, I don't know. Say hello to all the old places. The university letter won't be important. I'll deal with it when I come home. Love from us both, Janey.

I didn't call because Georges and I had had our first real quarrel and I knew my mother would sense immediately that something was wrong. We had often argued, Georges and I, but this was different. By forcing me to choose my future, he had stripped away the cloak of pretence, leaving me naked and ashamed.

I had woken in the night with stomach cramps. The curse, I told Georges, but because I had simply translated word for word he hadn't understood. '*Ah, tes jours*,' he exclaimed at last, his disappointment plain. 'I should take you to see a doctor.'

'*Mais c'est normal.*'

He laid his head on my stomach. 'Nonsense. *Baiser comme ça sans faire un seul bébé.*'

He still didn't know I was taking the Pill, a deceit I justified (when I thought of it at all) by reference to Georges's Catholicism and my dislike of papal interference in choices that were no business of theirs. But the threat of intervention by the French medical profession provoked a small crisis of guilt and to hide my distress, I pleaded with him to spend the day with me at the farm. I was planting out seeds for the spring harvest, a task we could more easily accomplish together.

'There's little point. We won't be here in the spring.'

'I know. But I want to leave some mark of our time here. A sign . . . It'll make me feel better, please.'

Reluctantly, Georges agreed. He said that, if we starved, he could always blame me.

Just like old times it was, weeding and hoeing then dropping a thin line of seeds into the stony earth. Georges worked hard all day, renouncing his usual siesta and even offering to make lunch. By evening, he announced we both deserved a drink and after a quick hose-down he carried our chairs to the last patch of sun, over by the cornfields, and a carafe of sharp white wine from the cooler.

We sat and drank as the sun went down behind the fields,

talking of this and that, of what we would do the next day, and the next. Then I happened to mention that classes resumed in less than a month. Sooner or later I would have to return home. My chance remark dropped like a stone.

Georges said, 'I don't want you to leave. Not now. You belong here with me.'

'Look, Georges, we've talked this over before. You know the reasons. I finish what I start. Let me get my degree first. You know it matters to me.'

'Don't you ever consider what matters to me? I've been thinking a lot these last few weeks. We should move to Le Mans. I have already spoken to a friend up there. He knows of someone looking for a driver. Not one of the big boys, that's why they'd take a risk with me. I'd have to make my mark pretty fast, soon I'll be too old. If we wait another year . . .'

'You could always go on your own.'

'No, Janey. If you value what we have, we go together. On my own, I know exactly what will happen and that will be the end of you and me. I thought you were happy here.'

'I am. Oh, I don't know. Don't you sometimes feel that none of this is real? Like we're playing games, you and I. We've got to go back sooner or later. Face up to things again. We've proper work to do, both of us, while this . . .' My sweeping gesture embraced the house, the garden, the harvested fields beyond.

'It's real enough to me. I don't know what you want any more. I don't know who you are. I sometimes wonder if you know yourself. Look in your heart, Janey, assuming you've still got one. Or has it become one of these?'

He picked up a stone which he flung into the fields, disturbing crows among the stubble.

I felt my mouth go hard. On receiving no other sign he

141

said angrily, 'You're the one who's playing games. You say you want to learn, but you don't seem to be making much progress on that precious essay of yours.'

'It's a dissertation, not an essay. There is a difference, you know. Dissertations require *much* more thought.'

'I never see you read. Most of your books are still packed away. I've seen them.'

'I read when you're not here. The days when you go off and leave me alone.'

'That's the point, Janey. When I'm here, when we're together, you don't need them any more. Your French is as good as the next, better than mine, better than Sylvie's.'

'Ah, Sylvie. I wondered when you'd come to her. You're missing her, is that it? The last night in the villa, before we got slung out. I heard you in there, in Sylvie's room. You must think I'm an idiot, to carry on like that with me in the house.'

'I was too drunk to notice what was going on. We all were.'

'Jean wasn't. He heard, too. That's why he started the fight.'

'You don't understand men. They have certain rights, certain territories that belong to them.'

'And you were poking about in his.'

'Don't talk like that. You know I don't like it. Sylvie took whatever came her way.'

'I know. Like a pin cushion. That doesn't excuse things. You could have waited till some other time, when I wasn't there.'

'Would that have made it any better? You really are a fool, a bigger fool than I thought. Look, Sylvie took me in there. I was drunk so I followed her. We didn't get far, Jean saw to that. If you must know, she was trying to suck me off.

OK, OK, so I'm not particularly proud of myself. That has nothing to do with us, Janey. Don't drag us into the dirt. What we have is precious, you and I. But things can break. *Ça peut casser, tu sais.*

'On the contrary,' I said, in a voice that wasn't mine, 'this has everything to do with us.'

Through the scorched sunflowers at the edge of the field I watched a truck winding its way along the road, its progress heralded by swirls of dust. Monsieur Caron back from market at Châtellerault. The truck's engine rattled noisily. Georges placed his glass on the ground.

'If you go home now, then it is finished between us. You understand that, don't you, Janey?'

Words dropped like pebbles down a well. Plop, plop. Already I was seeing his face as a memory.

'You are making me choose?'

'It's not a question of choice. These are facts, Janey. I tell you what will happen.'

'You're right, of course. We can't go on like this.'

His face was slipping into the cracks, a face I had moulded with my hands, the clumsy tools of my apprentice love.

'I knew you would never stay, right from the beginning.'

I was standing barefoot on the earth, holding his head to the barren curves of my body, feeling the bristly curls between my fingers. I've watched blind people do it, seeing through their hands, imprinting another's image on the celluloid of their unseeing eyes. In the sadness of parting we belonged to each other more than we had ever done, his head resting in the angle of my hip, his hands pressed around my waist. The stirrings of reproach – I couldn't bear that, or his hurt.

'You should trust me more,' I said gently. 'I'll come with you if that's what you want. The rest – it doesn't matter any more. Please, Georges, trust me now. I couldn't bear to lose you, you know that, don't you?'

'You promise you won't go back?'

'Of course. If that's what you want.'

His face felt wet. So did mine. Tears of shame and relief. How could I treat him like this? But I used the only words that could possibly restore his faith in me. Later we'd have time for meanings, interpretations. Now I needed words strong enough to heal our mutual distrust. Words that would sear our wounds and deliver us to silence.

We went inside. I felt as if I walked on glass. Delicious shivers of pain. My soles pierced by fragments sharp as knives. Blood on the sheets, swirling like slime. I straddled him on the bed, felt his hard body between my legs, his body that continued to surprise me. Then I did what Sylvie had done. Took him in my mouth. Breathed that warm, chickeny smell. Felt him stirring within me, the throbbing of his veins: this was good, for both of us. I waited until I saw the whites of his eyes, his voice calling my name – *Génie, Génie*. Yes, I knew how to please him now, when to advance and when to hold back, when to give of myself and when simply to receive. He had taught me well in the short time we had been together and now it was my turn to surprise him, lying on my front hunched over the bolster and guiding him with expert hand, his cock sliding in and out of my fluffy black *chatte*, and if he mistook my purrings of pleasure for the final submission of my will was it my fault or his that I was really saying goodbye?

The minute we had finished in bed Georges sat me down to write to my tutor, informing him that I wouldn't be returning in the autumn. I was to marry very soon, a

144

Frenchman by the name of Georges Delvaux, and after that I wouldn't have time. Sorry to let you down like this, but thanks for all you have done. I was never a model student: I hope you understand.

Too bad if you don't, said Georges, laughing up one side of his face and insisting that I translate each word before I wrote it down to avoid misunderstandings between us. He stood behind me as I wrote the envelope (in capital letters) then ordered me to dress and drove me in the dark to the post, suggesting that if I left it till morning, I might change my mind. He even frogmarched me to the letter box, 'just in case'.

Poor Georges. He wasn't there when I sealed the letter, trusting in my sudden change of heart. He didn't know the envelope contained a blank sheet of paper – the other I destroyed when Georges got the car from the barn. I wondered what my tutor would think if he recognised the handwriting on the envelope. Too bad. I could always invent some plausible excuse.

In retrospect, I find this repugnant but the skein of my emotions had become too tangled to expect better. I loved him and knew it wouldn't last, all in the same breath, so I was doing no more than any other: having my cake and sleeping with it as Kate would say.

FIFTEEN

Those last weeks passed in the fractured clarity of a dream. Nothing connected but neither did it *not* connect. I had given Georges my word. He had watched me post it in a letter box. Certain, now, that I would become his wife he acted as he had at the start, funny and wise, the clown with a silent guitar. I shut my mind to any thoughts of pity. Sooner or later I would leave. How or when was left to chance. A reason, you may think, for what I did in the end. Please believe me when I say I seek merely to understand, not to excuse the shabbiness of my behaviour.

Kate sent me a postcard as soon as the Gilberts had forwarded my note. She had found a place to stay at Hossegor on the Atlantic coast, living with a family who rented out their spare bathroom. They gave her a camp bed next to the bath. Before she left Bordeaux the police had come looking for me at the Gilberts'. Everything went as planned. When they heard about the stolen books, they said that explained everything. As far as they were concerned, the matter was closed but Monsieur Gilbert was *furious*.

Georges came into money. On receiving a letter he went into town, broke as usual, returning several café-hours later, his jacket fat with banknotes. We laid them on the bed in separate piles. Enough to last us through the year, he said. I said, 'Fine,' assuming the money had come from Jean. Didn't ask, though. Didn't want to know.

I gave up gardening. When pressed by Georges, I said there wasn't much point as we wouldn't be there to taste the fruits. We were moving to Le Mans, weren't we, as soon as he had prepared the ground? Unable to watch the flowers die he took to watering himself.

Instead of gardening I wandered the farm. A bitch had given birth in one of the barns. The mongrel pups mewled in a heap, eyes tight as slits. Madame Caron, finding me in the hay, said I could keep one myself once the puppies were weaned. I signalled my choice: a brown-and-white pup that always heaved itself to the top of the pile.

Out beyond the farmhouse I was attacked by geese and sought refuge behind the rabbit hutches which old Farmer Caron kept stacked in a field. Now that his sons had taken over the heavy work, he had too much time on his hands. We often used to meet and talk. I liked him very much. He had a sly twinkling face, flushed purple, a gleeful way with words. Invariably we talked about the weather. Hailstones at Preuilly-sur-Claise big as dumplings. Electric storms down towards Chauvigny. 'They say, Madame, you can plug your *télé* into the sky. He, he, he.' He offered me one of the rabbits. 'Madame will skin it for you if you ask nicely.' I didn't want that.

Sunflowers withered in the fields. Six feet tall and dying where they stood. Georges told me that's how they did things: you had to wait for the plants to die before harvesting began.

The summer ended for me the day we drove to Le Limousin. I knew that instinctively the moment I stepped outside. An unmistakable chill in the air lingered until the sun climbed over the outhouse roof. Deep blue sky. Chauvigny's storm clouds hadn't come here.

At breakfast Georges proposed an excursion to the château where he had purchased the statue of the dancing girl. The chatelaine lived alone. She might have other things to sell. I said I wasn't sure if I wanted to pay her a visit but an outing would do me good. The farm had begun to feel like a prison.

On the way we stopped off to visit the ruined castle at Angles-sur-l'Anglin then meandered along the course of the Gartempe to the frescoed church at St-Savin and down past the falls of Portes-d'Enfer. After that we found ourselves in wooded hills, cool and green after the summer's heat of the plains. The landscape enchanted me but there was an unbearable quality about it, too. It made me think of home.

Towards late afternoon we arrived at Les Sablons. Georges drove straight to the château, stopping the car outside a rusting iron grille. Nailed to the gatepost was a hand-painted sign: PROPRIÉTÉ PRIVÉE, it said, and another – seasoned by wind and rain – CHIEN MÉCHANT.

'If you believe that,' said Georges, 'the countryside is overrun by naughty dogs and half the towns, too.'

I got out. The gates were fastened with a huge padlock that hadn't been properly shut: it came away in my hands. Through the gates I could see the dirt track winding out of sight between heavily wooded banks and in the far distance, the peak of a turret rising above a thin line of fir trees.

Trespassers will be prosecuted. Private. KEEP OUT. I thought of a time long ago, when I was still a girl. The castle at Rockingham: how old was I then, ten, twelve? We had planned a raid on the castle chicken coops, myself, my brother Martin, a gang of boys from the council estate

148

on the outskirts of our Northamptonshire village. The gamekeeper found us before we got very far. He had his gun with him. I'm sure he meant simply to give us a fright but one of the youths was hit in the thigh, a boy called Fat Willy who screamed his head off while the rest of us ran away. Martin tripped into the lily pond, I had to fish him out myself, and when we got home I made him swear on all the things he held most dear, the Bible, his rabbits, my trust, that he would never give us away.

We never did tell. Mum thought Martin had fallen into a neighbour's ornamental pool. Dad – I'm not sure what he thought but a week or so afterwards he read us a piece from the local newspaper about a marauding gang of youths who had broken into the castle grounds, causing considerable damage. One of the boys had been accidentally shot while being apprehended by a Mr Bootle, a Mr James Bootle, the gamekeeper, obviously. Dad turned the story into a moral: what happens when you do the wrong thing, set foot on other people's land, take what isn't yours. People get hurt, he said, and not just you. Mr Bootle might well lose his job. That was the only part of the story I chose to ignore. Otherwise, Dad was wrong. You could get away with murder as long as you didn't tell.

Georges called from the car. '*Ça va, toi?*'

'Fine,' I said, 'but we really shouldn't be here. This is private land. We'd be trespassing.'

'She asked me to come back. You should see the stuff she has in there.'

'We don't need money. You said so yourself, we've got enough to last for months.'

'This is for you, Janey. To set us up in Le Mans. That costs, you know.'

149

'You said the statue was mine, the one that came from here. Then you took her away.'

'You continue to keep accounts, I see. If she means so much to you, I can always get her back.'

'Is it really that simple? Oh, never mind.'

After pushing open the gates I waited for Georges to pass then clanged them shut again. In the car, he leant towards me, slipping his hand into my knickers as he kissed my upstretched neck. I felt the familiar surge, made more potent by the fact that we weren't supposed to be here. He was pushing me into the back when I slammed my legs together and said regretfully, 'No time, really. Someone might see.'

'You don't want?'

'It's not that. But here – we shouldn't.'

'It has never bothered you before.'

'Don't force me, please. I'm sorry.'

'Sorry for what?'

'Nothing.'

He sighed. I kissed his disappointed face.

We straightened our clothes then Georges drove slowly up the track, rutted with black mud from recent rain. The car made a low purring sound. No one would hear our approach and if they did we could say we were invited guests. Spindly trees on both sides cut out the light. Georges seemed distant, his jaw set in a way I didn't like.

It was only when we made the last turn and found ourselves in the sweep of the carriage drive – sanded here, and raked – that I saw the long, turreted outline of the château with its jumble of outhouses and two wings swallowed by trees. In front of the house the drive swept round in a wide circle, enclosing what had once been a lawn. The grass had turned into a meadow. Someone had scythed a path to an overgrown fishpond at the centre then retreated elsewhere.

Georges stopped the car and we sat listening to subdued piano sounds from somewhere inside the house. Suddenly they stopped, mid-phrase.

'What are you thinking?' he asked, reaching for my hand.

I pulled it away before he could touch me. 'Nothing much. *Des bêtises.* Thoughts that go round and round.'

I watched from the car as he mounted the stone steps. At ground-floor level the windows were all shuttered. The cracked tinkling of a bell echoed inside. The place seemed empty. Perhaps I had imagined the piano. He rang again. Still no response. He tried the door – it was locked – then walked backwards down the steps, hands in pockets, looking up at the windows of the first floor.

'There's no one here,' I called from the car. 'Let's go home, it's getting late.'

'Wait. They say she never goes out, the old woman.'

'Who says? Georges, I don't like it. You saw the sign. Please, I think we should leave.'

'We can't give up now. She'll be in there somewhere, surrounded by her treasures. You won't believe how beautiful they are. Paintings, silver, porcelain, she must have a stack of jewels. Deaf as a pot, that's her problem.'

He rattled the shutters to one of the ground-floor windows which soon came away. Next he pushed against the window frame. He was wearing driving gloves. I felt a growing unease. If Georges knew the woman was inside, why was he trying to force entry? Someone was bound to come. She must have a maid, or a handyman.

151

I got quickly out of the car, glancing upwards as I hurried towards him. Georges, stepping back from the flowerbed, did the same.

A woman looked down on us from an upper window, a very old woman. Her shrunken face behind the curtain was hidden by a mess of shrivelled hair.

Georges cupped his hands to his mouth. 'It's me again, Madame,' he shouted, striding over to stand directly below her window. 'This time I bring you my wife. She asked especially to meet you. Would you care to let us in?'

The woman half-smiled then shook her head.

'Don't be shy, Madame. I have something for you.' From his back pocket he pulled a wad of notes which he waved towards the window. I found his performance obscene.

She hesitated.

He stuffed the notes away.

'Please let us in, Madame. I told my wife all about you. But you must hurry. We can't stay long.'

He walked very slowly towards the car, motioning that I should do the same.

The curtain fell shut.

'Georges,' I whispered, 'is this right?'

'She'll soon come down, don't fret.'

As Georges opened the car door for me we heard the rattling of keys. The sound of bolts being drawn. The hinges needed oil. Everything about that place was falling apart.

The woman appeared on the steps leaning on a stick. She looked very frail, brittle legs poking into carpet slippers, a navy pinafore worn over everyday clothes.

Georges embraced her as if he were family. She seemed to expect it and passed me her hand. Spotted with age, it felt bony and cold.

'Are you going to invite us inside?' asked Georges, a greasy smear to his voice.

She gave a senile little giggle then turned in the doorway. Down her back hung a long disorderly plait. *'Entrez, tout le monde.'* Her voice was pitched high like a girl's.

I followed her into the hall. Georges squeezed my arm. The shutters to the hall were closed. An impression of dark panelled wood, polished corridors leading off to left and right, two sweeps of an ornamental staircase that joined at the mezzanine.

'Come this way, please.' Beckoning to me, she hobbled off down the corridor to our right.

Georges held me back. 'She's taking us to the drawing room. I've seen the stuff in there already. Not bad but I'm sure there's better to be had. If she gives you the chance, wait in there. Say you need a rest or something. She'll respond better if I see her on my own.'

'Georges . . .'

'The way she carried on last time, I think she likes to tease.'

At the door to the drawing room the woman waved impatiently.

The room stretched the whole of one wing, grander than I had expected from the outside. We stepped into a pool of light from the open shutter. At the far end, across a sea of stiff-backed settees, I could dimly make out a carved stone fireplace beneath a solid gilt-framed mirror that stretched up to the high ceiling. Other mirrors reflected our images around the walls. My face looked unnaturally brown.

'So you like my little room?' she asked in her squeaky voice. 'They do too. Nothing changes in this house, they have me to thank for that. When I go, I shall pass it on intact. But they must take me out of this house feet first before I shall let them remove a single thing. Bah, families. Every time they visit they ask me to leave. They have a cottage for me somewhere . . .' She waved her hand towards the window. 'Only in a box, that's what I say. Let them rot first. And you, Madame, you have children?'

'Me?' Her question startled me. Surely I looked too young? 'No, not yet. Later, I'm sure.'

'First they break your heart. Then they throw the pieces in a barrow and cart it off to market. They're all the same, daughters, sons. *Mercenaires*, all of them. You will find it out for yourself one day. And when you do, remember it was I who told you what to expect, the chatelaine of Les Sablons.'

As she spoke, she twitched the corner of her pinafore. I struggled for something to say. Her bitterness left no chink.

The sound of footsteps, deep within the house. She looked at me sharply. 'That man of yours – is he one of them?'

'One of whom? Nobody sent him here, if that's what you mean.'

'My sons, my noble son-in-law, de Savigny, and the rest of the *canaille*?'

'No, Madame. I promise you. Georges, my husband, we came here for a drive. He said you might have something else to sell.'

'He knows I have nothing to sell. I cannot. The law forbids it: everything belongs to them. So how can I sell it to him?'

'But the statue, the dancing girl . . .'

The words were out before I could stop myself. I tried to make amends. 'Before you let us in, he showed you money. If you can't sell . . .'

154

Her face cracked into a pitying smile. 'That was a joke, my child. A harmless joke with a woman old enough to be his grandmother. Even I can *jouer la pute*. He's quite a fellow, that man of yours.'

Now she laughed at me openly. Her few remaining teeth were yellow and stubbly. 'So he told you I sold him the statue? Well, well. That's men for you. Same as children. *Mercenaires*, the lot of them.'

'Yes, he did.' I was close to tears. So Georges hadn't bought the statue at all. The man I loved, still loved, in spite of everything, was a common thief.

I said stiffly, 'I shall get him to return it at once. Or at least make some reparation. We don't have it any more, I'm afraid, but he said he could easily get it back. I'll see that he does. I'm sorry for all the trouble we have caused, Madame.'

Her cackling turned to a hoot. She wiped away the tears that trickled down her face. Then she said, 'You still haven't understood, have you? I *gave* him the statue, child. If he told you he bought it . . . Well, that's his affair. And what he does with it, too.'

'You gave it to him? Why?'

'Because I like him. Because he made me laugh. Because he made me feel young again. You young people think you have everything. You forget that one day you will be just like us. Forgotten, worthless. That man of yours is different. You should treasure him. Better give it to him than let the vultures get their claws into it, don't you think?'

'I . . . suppose so. If that's how you want it.'

'You don't sound very sure. But then you don't know my sons, or that monster de Savigny. Now, we should go and find him, your husband. I want to talk with him again.'

'If you don't mind, I'd rather stay here.'

She smiled gracefully. It was the first thing I'd done right all day. 'That is very kind of you, child. I shan't detain him long.'

Her footsteps retreated into the house, and the tapping of her stick.

Dust clouds rose from the stiff-backed settee. I sneezed several times in succession. *Poussière, tout n'est que poussière* . . . I thought of all the other dusty rooms I had known. Large as a ballroom, it was, illuminated with thick, motey sunbeams at one end. The particles rose and fell in the light, coming to rest on an ancient klavier stacked with family portraits in silver frames.

The distant sound of minuets, a stately waltz, so faint I wondered if I heard them all. It felt as if I sat there for hours.

Generations crowded on to the klavier. So these were the vultures and the vultures' forebears, the woman herself when young. Her face, surrounded by a mass of fair hair, had a haughty expression that commanded respect. Yvonne de Galais without the freshness of beauty but with something just as precious: a belief in her divine right to do as she pleased. In another photograph I counted the sons at her side, six in all; a single, plump-cheeked daughter with none of her mother's grace. Standing apart from the others, her frock-coated husband held a disapproving monocle to his eye. Nothing recent to mark the passage of time, to pierce the illusion that she lived in the gilded promise of her youth before her daughter married the noble de Savigny, her sons turned into swine.

156

Among the portraits, I wrote our names in dust. Janey Wilcox. Georges Delvaux. I crossed them out and sat with my back to the door.

The castle sleeps; holds you fast within its opiate spell. *La belle au bois dormant*, waiting for a kiss. Except your prince is occupied elsewhere.

The longer you sit the more conscious you become of faint scurryings, indeterminate sounds that could be mice or human feet, the cracking of seasoned wood. You don't like it, do you? Neither do I. The place makes your fearful heart jump like a bean and you experience a childish indignation that he should bring you here and then abandon you so totally. Where is he? What is he doing with her, the woman he called *bidoche*, knacker's flesh?

Careful, now, down the panelled corridor towards the hall. Gaps in the shutters make a slanting grille of light on the floor. The front door is oak, bolted from the inside. You consider the possibility of escape but then you remember the woods that surround the château on all sides. Woods make you *nervous*. Freedom exists theoretically, at best.

Upstairs, that's where he went. That's where she followed him. If you want to find out what is going on . . . The choice is yours.

The stairs creak as I mount the treads, sliding my back against the grease-stained wall. I have taken the right-hand branch of the staircase. The left would have served me just as well. Choices, choices. The heels of my cheap white sandals catch in the threadbare runner. Brown toes extrude between the straps.

At the top, where the two staircase wings join, the corridor extends to left and right towards a square of light

157

at each end. Half-light, really. I take a few hesitant steps to my left. A single piano note stops me dead. It comes from the opposite direction. Not a definite sound; rather the memory of an echo that reverberates deep in my brain but in the *wrong part*. The effect is like smelling colours or hearing the taste of rain. Disoriented, I strain to catch other sounds that might direct me towards my goal. A cooing of wood pigeons under the eaves; a distant (real? imagined?) squeaking, creaking, the kind of sound made by two wires scraped one against the other or springs rhythmically compressed, krik–krik–kriiiik, but fainter.

Passing quickly towards my right I see a picture has been lifted from the wall. Its space – half a metre square, perhaps more – is marked by a dark rim of soiled paintwork. The remaining portraits belong to no noteworthy school, goitred men with blustery cheeks and good bourgeois wives (daughters, sisters), mouths tight as sphincters.

The squeaking has stopped. Feeling more confident I weave my way between heavy furniture pushed at intervals against both walls, mahogany chests and hideously ornate wardrobes, Second Empire style.

Bedrooms, bathrooms, vast claw-footed baths, wooden chairs stacked one on top of the other, enough to fill an entire Assembly Room, dust-sheeted nursery, a box of broken toys.

I have almost reached the cobwebbed window at the far end. Thick velvet curtains, burgundy faded to puce, tied back with mangy gold tassels. One (open) door remains.

She is sitting on a narrow bed, her back to the door, silhouetted against sky. Low gurgling sounds as she rocks herself backwards and forwards, clutching a frizzy black object that bobs between her knees. It looks like a long-haired chihuahua. Her dress hangs in folds from her spine, flesh-coloured. Where is her pinafore?

The woman turns her head. She must have heard my step at the door. Her face looks throttled; whitish-blue. Wild staring eyes. Blood rushes to my ears. I feel suddenly sick. That sound like an undead cry. Her throat or mine?

I think: this isn't happening. Not to me, it isn't. Not to anyone.

Footsteps from the floor above, moving fast. Down towards the grand staircase. Two feet or four? Impossible to tell. Once or twice the person (persons) barges into the furniture.

A thumping down the stairs.

The woman is old and frail. She can't possibly keep pace. No sound of her stick.

I start rattling off the months of the year, backwards. December, November, October . . .

A moment's pause. The footsteps waver then veer towards this room. The tramping of feet on wooden floors. September, August, June, no, July . . .

The door bangs open. I force myself to turn round. He stands in the doorway, a brown-paper package under his arm. His face looks hard and mean. The package is fastened with string. One end flaps against his shirt.

'Georges, what have you done? The old woman . . . Where is she?'

'She's taken ill. She can't come down right now.'

'Then we should call for help.'

'No phone here. Come on. If we leave now, I can telephone from the village.'

'Can't I see her? I could stay with her while you go for help.'

'She won't let you near. It's nothing, really. I'll get her a doctor. Quick.'

He dragged me by the elbow into the hall, swearing as I pulled myself free and swung my fists at his chest. Called me a cunt, I think.

At the front door he ordered me to draw the bolts.

'I think we should stay.'

'*Putain de merde*. Just go, can't you?'

He pushed me through the door.

I looked back at the house. Upstairs, the windows were blank. She wasn't watching any more, *la vieille*, like she had been when we came and when I . . . when I went upstairs. What were they doing, the pair of them? Could I trust him to tell the truth? He made her laugh. That's what she told me. Made her feel like a girl. *He, he, he*. Laughing can kill, if you've lost the habit. She can't have laughed for years.

Tyres swished through the long grass. Georges had misjudged the curve. We started to swerve then the engine died. Grass came up to my window. He tried again. The wheels were stuck in mud. The harder he revved the engine, the faster the tyres spun round without holding fast.

'You drive,' he said.

'Me? I can't.'

'You have a licence?'

'Yes, but it's months since I tried. The controls, they're on the wrong side.'

Brusquely, he explained the pedals and got out. I moved to the driving seat. He was bending his weight against the bumper, out of sight. Sitting stiffly at the wheel, I engaged the gear and jerked my foot on the accelerator.

160

'*Doucement*,' he shouted. I pressed the pedal more slowly, felt the car give a buck then slide forwards on to the track where I should have stopped for Georges but the thrill of control forced me on towards a line of trees. The wheel oscillated in my hands. Georges was running by the other door, banging on the window. I slowed to let him in. His face and shirt were spattered with mud. I felt a rush of elation as we bounced down the track.

At the gates he ordered me to stop.

'Can't I drive through the village?'

'No,' he said. 'The way you drive – the *flics* would be on to us right away.'

The first village passed in a fuzz of stone walls. I reminded Georges of his promise to telephone for help. He glanced at me quickly. 'Next café we see.'

It was twenty minutes at least before we found a place to stop. I noticed the name: Café des Sports.

'Wait here.'

'I'm coming too.'

At the bar I asked for a Coke and a *jeton* for Georges. The phone was down some steps by the WC. I couldn't follow him there so I stayed at the bar. He was talking, all right, but to whom?

As we approached the plains of Poitou, I asked him about the package which he had hidden on the back seat under the blanket. He said it was a painting, a pretty valuable painting, eighteenth century. The old woman had sold it to him when they went upstairs and just as she was wrapping it up she was taken ill. Heartburn. Nothing too serious, he hoped.

I said, very quietly, that I didn't believe him. She had told

161

me already about the statue. That nothing in the house was hers to sell.

'OK, OK. She gave it to me, if you must know.'

'Because she likes you, I suppose?'

'That's right.'

'Or because you did something she wanted?'

He shrugged.

'But it doesn't belong to her. So even if she did give it to you . . .'

'If, Janey?'

'It wasn't hers to give. Whether you took it or whether she gave it to you – it's the same thing, really.'

'There's a world of difference between giving and taking. You should know that by now.'

I made my voice very small. 'What kept you so long, up there?'

The car swerved slightly. He must have taken his eyes off the road.

'Up where?'

'In the château. With the old woman.'

'You really want to know? I will tell you if that's what you want. But remember: truth hurts. I think you know that just as well as I do and besides, it isn't always important.'

He was right, of course. If he told me what he had done to the old woman I would have to face facts and facts are nasty. When you know the facts you must *do* something about them. You are what you make yourself, et cetera.

I kept looking ahead, praying that my tears wouldn't show. A lorry approached from the right. His priority. Georges made no attempt to stop.

'You're not very brave, are you?' he said in a voice devoid of triumph.

On the seat he reached for my hand. I moved too late. After a slight tug I left it under his on the seat and kept my eyes looking straight ahead, face all moony.

For over an hour he held my hand and I didn't have a hand. The stump was severed below the elbow. Every now and then it gave a slight twitch, like a *mutilée de guerre*.

We didn't speak again until we reached the farm.

As Georges parked in the barn I told him I wished to have nothing whatsoever to do with the painting. How he had come by it was his business but I wouldn't allow it past my door.

Georges put up an eloquent defence. He said the painting was more beautiful than anything I could ever have seen, more beautiful even than the bronze ballerina.

'Here, let me show you,' he said, tearing off the brown-paper wrapping and holding the painting up to the light.

I felt my chest go tight. Yes, it was beautiful all right, its luminous surface cracked with age. A trio of naked shepherdesses danced to the music of Pan against a sombre landscape of wooded hills. Darkness and light in stark contrast: the dark like Rembrandt, the light epiphanous.

I told him to wrap it up straight away and leave it in one of the outhouses. There were rats, so what? He knew what he could do.

SIXTEEN

My response to the painting was instinctive and total. I wanted nothing to do with it. I saw it for ten, fifteen seconds, no more, yet its details remain stamped on my mind: the leer on the face of the Great God Pan, playing his infernal pipes at the edge of the forest; the distant manor house, picked out by a single shaft of light – a house sliding into decay like the château at Les Sablons; worst of all the dancers themselves, naked except for a billow of cloth that directed the eye to the plumpness of bare shoulder, softly curved buttocks and thigh, a corruption of flesh more menacing than Pan's cloven-footed lechery.

Whatever the precise cause of my distress I kept my resolve and after Georges had hidden the painting in the barn we never spoke of it again.

He must have known it was finished between us and yet we both lacked courage to confront the inevitability of parting and so we led a clockwork life of gestures and empty words, commonplace actions that disguised our private thoughts. In bed we continued to have sex, always in the dark so that we couldn't read each other's eyes. That's how I felt, at least. I can't speak for him.

Neither Georges nor I emerge with any credit; I see that now as I doubtless saw it then which explains why I

164

never told Kate what happened at the end. Like old Caron's rabbits, I waited for the final *coup*.

Georges took every excuse to drive into town, often staying away all day. His *bricolage* went with him piece by piece. The painting went on about the third or fourth day. I wasn't surprised to see it go though I did wonder how he might dispose of it. He had contacts, I supposed, fly-by-nights like himself who knew how to turn a shady trick to their advantage. The answer, when it came, should have been obvious.

Georges had left the cottage at dawn. I heard his car backing up the lane then went back to sleep. When I rose, much later, I found we had run out of milk and after wandering up to the farm, where Madame Caron told me the pup would be mine in a week, I went back home, made coffee, cut myself some bread – it was rock stale – and ate at the kitchen table, my back to the open door, reading a class book propped against the *cafetière*.

I felt him before I saw him, felt his shadow fall across the room. In that first second I knew who it was. Despite appearances I wasn't afraid.

My chair scraped on the flags. 'Welcome,' I said. 'I wondered when you'd come.'

He moved into the room, hunching his shoulders to avoid banging his head against the ceiling. I had never noticed how low the rooms were. Georges and I cleared them with ease.

He sat down across the table. I motioned towards the coffee-pot.

He helped himself without removing his gloves.

'How's Sylvie?' I asked in a voice unnaturally devoid of curiosity.

A slow smile worked its way across his ugly face. 'Same as ever. You know how these things are.'

I passed him a hard lump of bread. If he ate from my hand, I might give him whaat he wanted. If not, he could go to the devil.

'And Georges?'

'Not here. He won't be back for hours. You'll see.'

'Shame.'

He started to eat the bread, watching me all the time as if he feared I might try to escape. I wasn't going anywhere. Not now.

The coffee was cold. I got up to make some more. As I stood over the stove, waiting for the water to boil, I heard the scrape of his chair. He was standing behind me now. I willed myself not to move. His hands slipped round my waist, pulled me backwards towards him. He felt very strong. I couldn't resist, even if I had wanted to. But I didn't want to resist, that's what makes it hard. This ugly, giant of a man: I thought I was settling scores, striking back at Georges for all his nasty tricks when really I was doing this for me.

The hard rush of desire made me swing round. He didn't like me any better, I could tell from the way he started slowly to unbuckle his leather belt as if he wanted to beat the shit out of me. I wanted that too, oh yes, I wanted him to beat me until I begged him to stop.

Pushing him away, I ran next door. He stumbled after me, knocking into the furniture. The man had planks for brains. I stood my ground as he ducked his head through the doorway. The bed was far too short. He threw me over the side. Too fast. I was losing control. It wasn't meant to happen like this. I tried to slow him down. That only made things worse.

He had his hands at my throat, a bursting of stars, then it didn't –

Abruptly, I shut my notebook and stand by the window. Stephen is digging in the garden below. His manner makes me smile. He digs savagely like a dog desperate to recover a bone, resting every few seconds on his spade. I've noticed it in other things he does, even sex: frantic activity followed by a moment's pause while he regains his composure. In the garden, at least, his efforts bear fruit despite an indifferent colour sense that persists in planting blues next to reds and muddling different kinds of pink. By the time the flowers bloom it is usually too late to take remedial action. 'That's your department,' he says (ironically), 'you're the artistic one.'

Any moment I expect him to raise his head towards my window under the eaves. There: he's turned in my direction. Now he's looking straight up at my window. Why doesn't he smile? Perhaps he can't see me properly or maybe he's not looking. I shan't wave. He might think I want him inside.

It didn't happen like that. I have allowed an inexcusable lapse in concentration to distort my careful catalogue of events. The frustrations of my age, you might think (I continue to consider myself young) but really I must look elsewhere for its cause. I find it significant that I want both to blacken my actions – Jean never touched me and as for beating the shit out of me, I find that laughable – and to plant the suggestion that one more sexual peccadillo was all that counted in the end. What I did was worse than that, far worse. I might find this story easier to bear if I had betrayed Georges's trust in such a squalid, ordinary way.

★　　★　　★

After his second cup of coffee Jean disappeared for several minutes, returning with a large canvas bag which he placed unopened on the table.

'Georges passed something on to me, a painting.'

So that's what he'd done with it. Of course. Jean was just the man to find a buyer. Doubtless he was sent the statue and other pickings of value.

'Do you know how he came by it?'

The question lay between us on the table. Without knowing Jean's hand, I couldn't be sure what he wanted.

I shrugged. Maybe I knew. Maybe I didn't. He was often away, I said. There were dealer friends who called. Maybe he'd got it from one of them.

'I think you know more than that.'

To gain time I cleared the breakfast things off the table, filling the bowl with water from the yard. This made him mad.

'Come here,' he ordered. I dragged my heels at the door. 'Do as I say.' He started to rise from his chair. I felt it wiser to obey and sat down beside him. 'Georges does what he wants,' I said. '*Je ne suis pas sa gardienne*. I am not my brother's keeper . . .' He frowned impatiently. 'Look, if you're so keen to know how he got hold of it, why don't you ask him yourself? He'll be back sometime. Don't know when. These days he doesn't tell me much but he'll be back before dark. He's never spent the night away yet. There's always a first time, I suppose.'

I could see his brain clicking away and felt suddenly vulnerable. It might have been better if I had disguised the true state of affairs between us. I felt frightened then, for Georges and for me.

He shook his head. 'I need to know now. Georges has landed me in trouble. *La merde*: you know what I mean?

168

It's possible they took him too, in which case, *il peut se torcher le cul soi-même*. But if he knew where the painting came from, well, that changes things, doesn't it?'

'That depends.'

'Doesn't it?' he repeated.

'OK, OK. But I can't help. You'll have to wait for Georges.'

For a moment I thought he was going to hit me. I flinched. He reached into his jacket and passed me a cutting torn from a newspaper. The print quality looked bad. Clearly some local rag.

'Read it.'

The words bounced up and down. *Chatelaine of Les Sablons found dead in suspicious circumstances . . . following an untraced call to the authorities . . . died of a heart-attack . . .* So Georges had phoned. He wasn't as black as I thought. Without his call they might never have known. My fault for pushing him into it. *Objects of value missing from the estate . . .* The list went on and on: either Georges bled her dry or the vultures were trying to conceal their tracks, *mercenaires* to the last man. I recognised the painting, the dancing shepherdesses, the Italian bronze, but not the others. *Police believe an intruder . . . fingerprint experts say* . . . Christ, those are mine. Georges wore gloves, unless he took them off. Can't remember. His hand on the shutters, he was wearing them then . . . *grieving family gathered to pay their* . . . Hypocrites, they wanted her dead. She swore she'd leave feet first. Now they had her where they wanted her, dead in a box, while they fought each other for the loot . . . *experts believe that names written in dust . . . trying to identify . . .* Jesus fucking Christ . . .

My heart raced ahead of itself. How could I have been so *stupid*? But when I doodled in the dust, I didn't think she

169

might die. Was it really a heart-attack? Or was it something Georges did? I saw them together upstairs. No I didn't. That was something else. Did he strike her perhaps? It could have happened to anyone. She was old. Why did it happen to us? Her cackling rang in my brain. *I gave him the statue, child. If he told you he bought it, well, that's men for you.* She deserved better than this. If we hadn't come, she might have held them at bay for years, guarding the things that weren't hers, giving them to men who made her laugh, who made her feel desired. If the vultures had told the truth about the objects missing from the estate, then Georges was neither the first nor the last. If, if, if . . . But he did come last, didn't he? Georges was the one who made her laugh so much she finally croaked, unless he did something else . . .

I handed back the cutting. 'So? What makes you think Georges had anything to do with that?'

Jean folded it away then sat with his hands on the table. Butchers' hands in black leather gloves. He could have put them round the old woman's waist and still have room to spare. Snapped her in two like brushwood. Thank God he wasn't there. She wouldn't have found much to laugh about with an oaf like him.

'We both know Georges,' he said slowly. 'Stories, they repeat themselves.'

'What do you mean?'

I knew I shouldn't press further. But I couldn't stop myself. Sometimes you have to know, even when you don't want to hear.

'He told you about his uncle? When he was last in trouble?'

I shook my head. Felt my tears welling up again.

'*La pauvre.*'

170

The weight of his gloved hand on mine. Shiny leather like the seats of Georges's car. I didn't need his pity.

I said, 'You might as well tell me. I'm leaving anyway. I suppose it's that thing to do with his wife. He told me what the judge said . . . How he was the scum of the earth. I never asked for the details. Funny, isn't it, I don't know her name. Georges never told me, you see.'

'Wrong story, Janey. This happened afterwards. Georges was down on his luck – that bitch took him for everything he had. She's called Jocelyne, by the way. Poison. I always told him it would end badly. An uncle took him in, put him in charge of a garage he ran in town. His uncle the *garagiste*, I've met him a few times. A real *anarchiste*: stolen cars, laundering, false compartments, the lot. That's where Georges learned his tricks. One day, the uncle lent him a car, a Lotus. Very smart. Georges ran off with it, claiming it as a gift, money owed, you know how it goes. He thought his uncle would be too scared to go to the police but he was wrong. The car belonged to someone else – it gets complicated, you see. The uncle had no choice: he had to get it back. There was a fight, the police interrogated Georges but without proof there was little they could do. Georges shopped his uncle for all he was worth. The police had what they wanted at last. Georges was dispensable, chicken-shit.'

'So Georges was freed? I mean, he was never charged with any offence?'

'It didn't finish there. Tales, stories . . . He was locked up for his own protection. The uncle swore on oath that Georges had interfered with one of his daughters, a cousin. She was very young, eight, nine. The girl was no longer pure. *Dépucelée*, you know what that is? Georges blamed his uncle, claiming to have watched them at it one night

171

in the room she shared with her younger sister. The girl, I don't know what happened to her. It got very . . . messy. As far as I know, Georges escaped with a warning. That's Georges for you. He likes them young but *la petite frangine*, eight, nine? Even his friends think he's shit.'

So that was it. A squalid family feud. While I didn't for a moment believe the story about Georges and his cousin, all the rest rang true. Pushed into a corner, he was bound to fight mean. I had thought it an affair of the heart. That's what angered me most: not what Georges had done but the romancing I had made of it, culling my schoolgirl fancies second-hand from books, from Art, from Literature, while life carried on elsewhere.

Jean's revelations had finally cut me free. Books, literature, what did they know about *life*?

To prove to myself I had grown into a woman at last, I did the one thing I have grown bitterly to regret: I told Jean *everything*. About the bronze statuette that Georges had given me then taken away. About our visit to Les Sablons and what I might have seen upstairs: Georges with his snout up an old woman's *bonbonnière*. About her 'gift' of a painting and our subsequent flight. About his call from the café, presumably to alert the authorities. *Lovers love. Informers inform*: what else can they do?

'So he knew she was dead?'

'You'll have to ask Georges that. I never saw her. He wouldn't let me go up. He certainly knew that everything in the house belonged to the family, not to her. We argued about it on the way home.'

'You're sure of that? That Georges knew the painting wasn't legally hers? The rest, *je m'en fiche*.'

'Yes, Jean, he knew that though she gave it to him it wasn't hers to give. I'm certain of that, I promise you.'

172

'Good.'

Having concluded his interrogation he became unpleasantly brisk, telling me in simple terms what he planned to do. The canvas bag contained the painting, the one Georges had tried to hang round his neck. A contact had warned him off. There were still people in this business he could trust. He would leave the painting here in the cottage. I wasn't to touch it or he'd break every bone in my body. On quitting the farm – his car was parked up the lane – he would drive to La Roche-Posay where he would inform the gendarmerie. That left me about half an hour to clear out. He wouldn't give them my name unless I tampered with the painting, in which case, well, we'd see about that.

I felt very small and scared.

'Can't I come with you? I won't be any trouble. You could drop me where you like, anywhere. Just to give me a start.'

He didn't bother to reply.

'What if Georges comes back? Before the police arrive?'

'I leave that to you.'

At the door he fumbled in his jacket. I thought he wanted to give me the newspaper cutting. 'No, keep it,' I said. He walked back into the room, counting from a bundle of notes, several of which he laid on the table. When he was gone I counted them myself. Three hundred francs. So that was the price he placed on Georges's head.

We were driving along the open road. Fields of dead sunflowers on either side. Burning stubble from the corn. The engine's diesel fumes made me feel sick. At least its throaty rattle made conversation impossible. Then a car, the Gordini, appeared over the horizon in a flash of French racing blue. I had been expecting it ever since we left the farm. Old Farmer Caron saw it too. I could tell him to stop, flag down the car – there was still time – warn Georges against returning to the cottage.

The old man was looking at me, waiting to see what I would do. The car was advancing towards us, too fast, he'd have disappeared before Caron hit the brakes. I slid my head below the dashboard. The noise and smells got worse. After counting the seconds to a full minute I climbed back to my seat and we continued as before, bumping down the dusty road towards the outskirts of town. '*Ce sont des conneries,*' he shouted with an old man's twinkle to his eye.

SEVENTEEN

I have this recurring nightmare. I am about to embark on a journey, unplanned, and must pack my suitcases against the clock. I've had it since I was a child, since long before I went to France: what happened there has only made it worse. Each variant brings new terrors. Sometimes it's my passport I can't find; or I don't know what the weather will be like on the other side. Once I couldn't find my cases at all and had the humiliation of bustling like a bag-lady up the gangway of some luxury liner to mingle with crowds in full evening dress. I know it doesn't sound much but when I wake my skin is damp with sweat. Only Stephen appreciates how panicked I feel.

In my flight from the cottage I left a number of items behind: clothes, shoes, make-up, an old raincoat, several paperbacks. Nothing with my name on it, as far as I know, because they never came looking for me though I remained jumpy for days, weeks afterwards and couldn't hear the phone ringing without wondering if they had finally caught up with me. Mum blamed my nerves on the sudden – and, on my part, unexplained – break to my 'engagement' with Georges. Things hadn't worked out was all I said. Dad gave notice to his popsy. 'Improved my French no end,' he remarked with an air of regret.

★   ★   ★

Monsieur Caron drove me in his truck all the way to the station at Chatellerault, my bags bouncing about the back which was used to cart muck from one field to the next.

I used Jean's money to buy my ticket, intending to repay it one day but somehow I never did. The formalities were daunting. Jean might never have returned to the villa and sending anything that could be traced back to me was tempting providence.

In the train people near me changed places whenever they got the chance.

It was dark when the train reached Paris. I took the Métro to Rachel's without calling first. The door opened before I could ring. She didn't recognise me straight away, nor did André.

'Hello,' I said, feeling sheepish as I stood on their doorstep with my two mucky bags. 'It's me, Janey. I need somewhere to stay, just for the night. I'm on my way home.'

From the look she gave me, I could tell it wasn't convenient. 'Don't worry. I could always try a hotel. There must be a room, somewhere.'

André refused to countenance such a suggestion. As he carried the heavier of my two bags up the stairs he explained they were going out to the cinema round the corner. *Les enfants du paradis*, an old film but one of the best. I was welcome to come too. I said I was tired after the journey and if they didn't mind, I would much prefer to stay home.

Looking pointedly at her watch, Rachel said I could sleep on the sofa as they didn't have a spare room. She found me some bedding in a cupboard then she hurried André away.

The flat was very tidy, its aura of calm accentuated by snatches of conversation that drifted up from the pavement below, a woman's impetuous laugh, an argument between friends. André had replaced the bus ticket with a new portrait of Rachel, fully clothed, in a style both simple and direct. With her light-brown hair, her pert and pretty face, she smiled with a tenderness that sliced me to the core.

I made up my bed and tried to sleep. To avoid thinking of Georges I busied myself with lists, tasks, half-written essays, things I should do when I got back to England. It didn't work. Thoughts and images jostled in my brain. Jean Seberg's face in the closing frames of *Breathless, Qu'est-ce que c'est dégueulasse?* 'You're wearing silk socks with tweed.' René Descartes hunched, thinking, in his *poêle* that transmuted into the cast-iron stove at La Colombe. The adolescent in Arthur Rimbaud. Compare, contrast, *discuss*, dammit.

At the click of Rachel's key I switched on the light, eager for company. The three of us talked for a time. To my surprise, Rachel asked after Georges. Apparently Yves had spoken out in his defence after a disparaging remark from Hélène. (She had called him a melon.) Yves disagreed. He said Georges was the most original man he had ever met, a man with balls who knew the value of his own opinions and didn't give a damn what anyone else thought.

I explained that Georges and I had planned to marry but that was now unlikely. You needed more than balls to make a marriage work.

Rachel looked doubtful.

'Anyway, I don't think I'll see him again. We quarrelled, oh, you don't want to know the details. It just went wrong.'

'I am sorry,' she said, with a sincerity I found touching.

177

'I'd like to have got to know him better. Last time I didn't get the chance.'

'That was my fault. I don't know what came over me.'

'Yves has a theory: he thinks you got upset because you weren't able to say what you meant. On Tolkien, for instance . . .' I saw André give her a warning sign. 'Never mind,' she said quickly, 'it's all right now.'

We talked about going home. Rachel faced the prospect with equanimity. 'André insists I get a good degree. I can teach while he paints. For the first few years, I'll be the main breadwinner.'

'But I thought his reputation was already secure?'

'It is. Everyone agrees he'll be very big one day. In the meantime we have to live.'

'And what about you,' I asked. 'What do you want for yourself?'

'I want to make him happy,' she replied primly. 'That's good enough for me.'

The crossing was rough. I watched the cold grey waves, my stomach churning as we dipped up and down. I tried not to think. Sick as a dog, I felt. It wasn't hard.

The best thing was seeing Kate and hearing of her stay at Hossegor. The place sounded fun. She had quickly teamed up with a girl called Christine who attracted men like flypaper. As Christine already had a boyfriend Kate was able to pick and choose from the rest and made the most of her opportunity. She asked tactfully after Georges without pursuing that business with the books. I would tell her if I wanted to. If not, she wouldn't hold it against me. We talked of other things instead, about the ocean at Hossegor and life on the farm, about the Gilberts and Père

178

Caron, about the sweeping questions we faced in our final exams, questions of Art and Reality, of Illusion and Truth, of Albert Camus's one serious philosophical problem: whether Life was worth all the bother of being lived.

During that last year I saw a lot of Henry Marchfeld without finding it necessary to go to bed with him. He said France had changed me into a woman; a woman, moreover, to whom he could relate as a friend. I thought he'd changed too. He didn't laugh quite so much. We met regularly for coffee at the Berkeley and sometimes for lunch when he confided the mishaps of his complicated love life without demanding similar confidences from me.

My hard work over the final year earned me a good degree, a 2:1, almost a First. My tutor said my dissertation on Rimbaud was one of the best he had read in years. 'Original' was the word he used. 'Words into Winchesters, it all fits, Miss Wilcox. Thank you for showing us how.' Knowing where the idea had come from, I smiled nicely and said I was glad he was pleased.

I would like to think that my shoddy treatment of Georges gave rise now and then to the sly stirrings of conscience. I could have saved him from Jean's trap. Asked Monsieur Caron to stop the truck the instant we saw his car. At the very least written him a note. I hadn't even said goodbye. It seems monstrous to me now, perfectly, utterly, monstrous but I believe I am correct in saying that I found a way of stifling any stray bubble of remorse before it broke the surface of my conscious mind. I dropped my French experiences to the bottom of the tank, to the estuarial slime off the charted coasts of memory, allowing the silt of daily life to place an impenetrable seal between what I was then and what I had become, a self-willed amnesiac who needed to re-learn the correct response to each fresh situation. That's nice. That's kind. Stop it, you're hurting me. So this is what they mean by 'love'?

Do you know how dark it is at the bottom of the ocean, how cold? The sun's rays do not penetrate here. Angler fish with dangling lights and spiked teeth. Gulper eels that trawl the sea-bed, open-mouthed. Absolute silence except for the noises of your own body, a hissing in your eardrums, visceral slurpings, a build-up of pressure at your temples.

But isn't there something else? A sound that comes from far away, tick, tick, softly at first, imagined, like the barnacled fuse on a deep-sea mine, tick, tick, tick, a sound you managed to ignore until the moment you saw that long-forgotten face on the TV screen, the man with dark wiry hair that hangs in rats' tails about his weasel face, the man whose unexpected re-appearance threatens to detonate your pusillanimity and with it the flimsy artefacts of your life.

Can you hear it too? It's getting louder every second. Tick, tick, tick, TICK, TICK. You want to scream but you can't scream underwater. No one would hear you even if you could.

A faint shifting of sand on the sea-bed. Fish tails slap against your face.

You feel the explosion before you see the flash, feel the walls of your body collapse inwards with a single thrust which you experience as the euphoria of release, the alchemical *separatio*, and you find yourself shooting upwards in a wild rush of water, black as night, through layers of cold and not-so-cold, Janey the human cannonball, a bursting in your chest as your perpendicular ascent flattens your arms against your sides, the surface fast approaching like a fluid glass plane, green and glinty. You hit it with a smack, rising high into the whiteness of air that suspends you in a mushroom cloud between sea and sky, blinded by sun – your own vision of eternity that lasts a scant few seconds before you are plunged back into the mountainous sea where you tread water frantically, tossed by the waves, your dead-man's eyes searching for a speck of land, a dove, a straw. And all around the sea runs darkly red.

EIGHTEEN

Day seeps into day. I find myself marking time, nerves locked on hold as I wait endlessly for something to happen – anything to break the silence of this lumbering house that squats beneath the lee of the hill, beyond the doctor's and the farm.

When we first moved here (from a bungalow in the village) I treasured our sense of living apart. Now I no longer know what to do with the brittle emptiness of long summer days and consequently waste much time floating in and out of the french windows, noting how the muslin curtains blow inwards in a light breeze, chasing shadows with my chair across the lawn.

Stephen's roses have faded already. Their scent this season failed to match expectations, a deficiency I blame on the year's exceptionally cold spring rains or else (more probably) the fault lies with me. My dormant senses struggle to remain in contact with even the most mundane objects. This deckchair, for instance, on which I am sitting: my mind knows it's a chair, my body plainly does too (I didn't sprawl in the grass on first sitting down) but could it be *something else as well?*

Stephen says I should seek medical advice if these feelings of unreality continue. He means well, I'm sure, though I can't help snapping back in return.

★   ★   ★

It would have been so easy to find him. A colleague in the French Department knows a girl whose brother works as a racing commentator for one of the French radio stations. Justin Langlois is his name. I am assured that Justin would be able to supply addresses, phone numbers, anything I asked. For several days I stalk the lawn in a state of high excitement then I think: what could we possibly say to each other after all this time? Life's a peach. Fine and dandy, how about you?

In my worst scenario I track him down to a café close to the circuit at Le Mans, a masculine sort of place where the talk is of cars, danger, the advantage of this manoeuvre over that, sometimes of women but not aggressively, more the shared tokens of male camaraderie. He sits in a corner, among a group of mechanics, looking just the same (I know that from the TV), his hairline receded into two bumps, peppered grey and white. Otherwise the years have given him no more than a slight scuffing like a coin that changes hands too many times. Thirty-five, forty-five, fifty-five: you wouldn't know, if you passed him in the street, how old he really is. Georges Delvaux, Janey Wilcox, names written – and erased – in the dust of an old woman's klavier.

Braving the jostling crowds I push my way to his table where I stand awkwardly, stomach knotted like a young girl, smiling as bravely as I can. He looks straight at me. From his air of puzzled indifference, the hint of a shrug he gives to the rat-faced youth beside him (his son Pascal?), I know with a sickening twist of the knife that he doesn't recognise me. Christ, that hurts. Whatever I did to him I deserve better than this.

I drop this particular line of enquiry and take to knitting instead.

★　　★　　★

I had almost reverted to normal when Kate called to say that Rachel had written to ask if we might visit a travelling exhibition at the National Gallery. The paintings, on loan from some provincial museum in France, included two of André's recent works: *Still Life With Water Bottle* and *Girl*.

'She says that André makes a point of never reading reviews. But she wants to know how the paintings look in London, and how the exhibition is being received.'

'I didn't know it was on.'

'Sounds pretty dull. I read something about it, some-where.'

'If she really wants me to go, why didn't she ask me herself?'

'She included you in her letter to me.'

'So? That means you're the one she really wants to go.'

'But you're the one with art history. It's your judgement she trusts.'

'I'm not sure about that.'

'Anyway, *I* want to see you, so please come. You can stay on a few days, if you like. I'll be working but there are things you could do. Rachel says there's talk of electing André to the Académie, in several years' time.'

I giggled. 'This hand has shaken the hand of an Academician . . .'

'Not "has",' corrected Kate, 'will one day have shaken. Future perfect. Rachel would want you to use the right tense.'

A couple of days before we were due to meet, Kate called again to say that Sam had gone down with chicken-pox and the office had sprung a meeting for the same day – a meeting in Birmingham, would I believe? – where the

184

printers had threatened a strike. Whichever she decided to do (and knowing Kate, Sam would come first), she couldn't be in three places at once and as she didn't know when she would next have a free afternoon would I mind awfully going to the exhibition on my own?

I did but there wasn't much I could do. Stephen had already bought my rail ticket and absolutely refused to claim a refund, insisting the change would do me good. Kate said I was still welcome to stay on for a few nights. Even if she went to Birmingham, she'd be back by five and Sam would love company: he was more bored than ill.

The morning I left, Stephen worked at home so that he could drive me to the station himself. My only visible sign of protest was to catch a later train than I might otherwise have done, leaving myself too little time to view the exhibition properly.

I was thankful to find the gallery almost deserted. Lukewarm reviews and the 'provincial' tag had deterred the usual crowds, which suited me fine. I left my raincoat in the cloakroom (they wouldn't take my bag), bought a gallery guide and the catalogue to send later to Rachel and spent an amusing half-hour hunting blind for André's two paintings. *Still Life with Water Bottle* was easy: it was the only *nature morte* included in the twentieth-century rooms and you could anyway see the water in the bottle.

Girl proved more elusive. I picked out two oils that each bore a passing resemblance to a younger version of Rachel, one in the manner of the late Impressionists, the other a straightforward example of seventies expressionism in which the torso of a young girl (divorced from its context by thick black lines) was severed by the frame. André Touvier was credited with neither.

185

Forced in the end to consult the catalogue, I was oddly annoyed to discover that André's 'girl' was a tiny (12 cm square) pencil-and-wash sketch of a child's face, pretty enough, that gained in depth the longer you stared at it. The face had no obvious connection with Rachel.

As I stepped back to examine it critically, an older woman in a flowery hat came and stood right next to me. She almost tripped over my bag. Before I could move away she turned and said, a little apologetically, that the picture reminded her of her granddaughter – not how she was now but how she might become. On the point of returning the confidence by telling her that the artist was a friend of mine – I had once studied French with his wife – I realised from the rheumy state of the woman's eyes that she quite possibly didn't *have* a granddaughter so I made one of those polite but cautious replies. 'Very nice,' I said without a trace of enthusiasm and hurried off.

The basement was even emptier than the exhibition galleries had been. I was looking for the stairs that connected with the cloakrooms, thinking I would slip out by the main exit then loop round to Charing Cross to catch a tube to Kate's. I must have misread the floor plan because the maze of interlocking rooms led nowhere.

Heading back towards the stairs, I glanced casually at the paintings hung on brick-coloured walls, all lesser works of the late seventeenth and eighteenth centuries, Italian, Belgian, French – not a period I know well and one for which I have little sympathy. Over-composed landscapes, peasant masquerades, obscure classical allusions, the gimcrack accoutrements of Picturesque conceits – quite dreadful, all of them. No wonder the aged security staff slumbered in their chairs. The lack of air down here made my head feel heavy like a football.

I might never have seen it.

By a bust of Alexander, I am startled by a loud coughing from the room to my right. The security guard has woken himself up, all teeth and whiskers and a dark black throat.

It is a moment I have replayed many times. Alexander swoons, eyes swivelled upwards. The coughing strikes as I pass towards the double doors, wrenching my head so that I am looking backwards over my shoulder. A jerking sound like the cranking of an old-fashioned musical box. Red walls stretched to a blur, blue wood, dark panelled doors. Seated guard in navy–blue uniform, whiskers smoked a nicotine yellow. Rows of neatly spaced paintings on either wall but fixed at weird angles on account of my particular perspective and there, fastened to the far wall, the only sharply defined object in the entire scene, a line of plumply dancing shepherdesses glistening pink and white like sugared mice. Good enough to eat, they look, as they cavort on the grass before the Great God Pan.

I open my mouth to speak. Leaves clog my throat. A moment of pure panic as I think I can't breathe.

The guard tugs at his seat, as if nailed down. Still coughing he gawps in alarm as I stumble towards the centre of the room and collapse on to a low wooden bench. Nausea rises up my throat. My breath comes in quick gasps. I am fiddling with the zip of my overnight bag. He reaches for something in his pocket. I want to tell him that I am really quite all right. I can't breathe too well, that's all.

He has located it at last, his walkie-talkie, and makes a show of rubbing it against his shirt. His eyes never leave my face. I stare hard at the painting. The guard stares at me. Disgust is the strongest emotion I feel but also a sickening fascination.

The canvas sucks me in. I am powerless to resist. This damned wind, it's like standing beside the nozzle of a giant vacuum cleaner that swallows me whole, one gulp and I am spun in a vortex of leaves, dead leaves, dizzily fast. Any second I'll be spewed like vomit across the floor. That'll take the shine off his shoes. Steady, now. Knuckles white as bones. Face, too, I shouldn't wonder.

When I think I can bear the whirling no longer I feel a scrape of canvas as my boundaries slip away. I am dancing naked on the grass to the music of Pan, mud from the riverbed sliding between my toes. The reedy pipes compel the movements of my dance, jerk my arms and bob my knees, sounds that come from the slimiest recesses of my belly as I slip shamelessly out of line, parading my sex like an oozing sore which I rub against the satyr's pelt and prepare to spear myself on the sweet stave of Priapus already thickening in anticipation. With the fingers of both hands I curl open the lips of my wound, stretch it wide as a cup, there, make it easy for the horny rod to slip inside and then – the moment I have waited for – I find *she* steps unbidden into frame. The old biddy spreadeagled on a sheet, knees apart, her *praline* pinned back to reveal the reeking cavities of an anatomical specimen.

That thing between her legs. What's black and furry and bobs up and down like an over-excited chihuahua? Georges's head, of course, snout in the trough – any trough will do as long as the price is right and she paid with stronger currency than mine.

The old woman's face as she looks towards the door. Sees me spying on the man clamped between her knees,

188

my husband (she thinks), the hired gigolo whose head she grasps with stringy hands, who makes her gurgle with satisfaction. Even I can *jouer la pute*.

The image unfolds in black-and-white. I might be sitting in the front row, a crick in my neck from craning upwards.

She cries out. Once? Twice? Helplessly raises her skinny arms. He thinks (how can I know what he thinks?) that she must be near to climax and she is, the old *boudin*. The shock of my appearance has overstrained her heart. She cries out one last time. Mistaking this for encouragement he works ever faster. Her face throttled purple as she struggles to speak. Mouth opens like a fish. No words come. Nor will they.

I have killed her, you see. You knew that already, I expect. So did I but deep down, below the waterline. Not pulled the trigger or thrust the knife or anything obvious like that. By the time she keels over I shall be sitting downstairs, choirboy hands folded in my lap. Calm as a tankful of piranha fish and none of this ever happened. I never came. I never saw. I never stooped so low as to trigger another's death and then to run away because I couldn't bear the consequences. Nothing to do with me, sorry. Blame Georges if you must but don't blame me.

The piping fades into silence.

I shake the sounds from my ears and look again at the painting. There's something not quite right. The dancing shepherdesses, exactly as I remember, and Pan blowing his pipes. But there, in the middle distance, a little comedy I hadn't noticed before: another dancer who attempts to flee a satyr's embrace. I honestly don't remember that. *Strange how memory plays you tricks*, I think, a trifle too calmly for the circumstances. A corpse is freshly exhumed and I find

189

myself fretting about some minor detail in a painting of mythological beasts and shepherdesses.

From a purely historical point of view no work of art is absurd; it is simply a piece of evidence. John Berger. *Ways of Seeing*, no, *Permanent Red*. Very apt, though he meant something else, I think. *Tant pis*.

I wipe my nose with my sleeve. The guard looks away. It wasn't like this, I want to shout out loud: *I simply don't remember*.

Stephen will know the answer, I think suddenly. His legal training will unravel for me the extent of my complicity. He'll want to know what happened, of course, and I don't want that.

I open the gallery guide. Each time I reach the nineteenth century I must return to the beginning. It might not be here: they can't include everything. The pages stick together. Tears blur my sight. It's like trying to see the sky from below the surface of the tank. Any second now the piranha fish will pick me clean.

At last I find the page I am seeking. The black-and-white reproduction gives no clue to the painting's extraordinary luminosity. That's why I couldn't find it before.

Les bérgères dansantes it says and above the title, in capital letters: *AFTER BOUCHER*. Without the golden light, you can barely make out the errant pair in the middle ground, the figures that obstinately refuse to take their place in a painting I last saw in the canvas bag Big Jean had placed on the kitchen table at La Colombe.

After Boucher. I read the notes to jump-start my brain. François Boucher, 1703–1770. Painter of nymphs and shepherdesses. Occasional book illustrator. The women's pose is borrowed from Watteau. They weren't there before, not in the version I saw. Three dancers, yes, a distant house,

Pan, no figures in the middle distance. Positive about that. Well, as positive as I can be after all this time. That means I saw the real thing, the real François Boucher, or *might* have seen it, assuming my memory tells the truth.

Jean put the bag on the table and threatened to call the police. It's probable he never did – he's a *blaguer*, that one. If he had called the police, Georges would have been arrested on suspicion of a whole string of charges: theft, rape, manslaughter, whatever they could make stick, and he wasn't arrested. Can't have been. He went to Le Mans as he always said he would. I know this for a fact because he sent me a wedding invitation, care of my parents' address, after I'd been gone a scant six months. The bride's name was Nathalie, can't remember her family name. That's life for you, the bitch.

After Boucher – the attribution leaves the question open: did I or did I not see the original? If this isn't the one I saw, what happened to the other, for God's sake, the one Jean brought back to La Colombe? Did they bury it together on the edge of the cornfield, always assuming the *flics* never came? Did they find a buyer after the stink had died down, splitting the profits between?

One step. Two steps. Slowly. I feel the guard's eyes on my back (I really do). Raise my hands slightly to prove I have nothing to hide. Stop by the cord that marks the limits of permitted distance, leaning ever so slightly forwards to shorten the gap.

Viewed in close-up, the most striking element of the painting is the colour and texture of the women's skin. Their bodies have the lustre of mother-of-pearl shading into pink, pink cheeks, pink buttocks, pink ears, pink toes. They are very fat, dimpled in all the wrong places. Prod them and your finger would disappear. There's something

191

grub-like and uncooked about them, in contrast to Pan's rich biscuit bake. The faces are less successful, superimposed with clumsy brush strokes. And though the manor house is adequately rendered I note that flowers have been overpainted in the foreground, apparently floating above the grass. Inferior technique, obviously. The artist – whoever he was – cannot have intended such close scrutiny.

I feel the guard relax as I return to the bench where I sit stiffly as a schoolgirl, bag on knee, staring straight ahead.

I don't like the picture, I decide. I didn't like it then and I don't like it now. Call it prejudice if you like but fat people have always made me feel uncomfortable. The artist's message is anyway far too obvious: the Dionysian attractions of sex (with a *satyr*?), the salaciousness of women, regret at the passing of time. The best I can say is that viewed from a distance, the light looks singularly attractive.

Already I start to feel better. I find I can look at the painting without the faintest tremor. A question of taste, pure and simple. This isn't my style.

After waiting several minutes to make sure I am really cured, I get up to leave as a youngish couple clatter into view. The girl wears a long red cardigan and black woollen skirt over scuffed black boots. I wonder if she realises her hair looks a mess. They come laughing into the gallery and stand arm in arm in front of another painting, a *fête galante* by Fragonard. The guardian yawns. The boy kisses the girl behind the ear. I don't think they've seen me so I say 'Excuse me' very loudly and walk past.

At the bust of Alexander I look back through the double doors. The girl has raised her left hand and points a forefinger at the Boucher. Her nails are painted burgundy red. The boy smiles glassily, embarrassed at something she has said. He knows the guard is watching them both.

Tension gains.

The clocks have all stopped at precisely the same time.

We are frozen together in a vacuum.

Then the girl breaks the spell by spinning a half-pirouette and coming to rest against the boy's shoulder. He starts talking, waving his arms. I have the curious impression of time unlocked. Even the guard comes to life, crosses his legs, uncrosses them, rises to his feet.

I walk through interconnecting rooms to the stairs, where I look back one last time. The door frames repeat themselves into infinity, getting smaller each time, like a trick with mirrors. Just as I mount the stairs the couple swing into sight. Their chattering voices follow me up to the Central Hall and out into the street. By the traffic lights below St Martin-in-the-Fields I remember I have left my raincoat in the cloakroom. I finger the token in my skirt pocket.

The lights have turned green. I cross the road away from the gallery, heading towards Charing Cross. I'll pick up the coat some other time, when I'm next in town. I don't need it now because I shall not stay with Kate after all. She will understand when I tell her why.

The lightness of my step makes me feel giddy, almost drunk, as I hurry towards the station. I want to see Stephen very badly. Before boarding the train I consider telephoning him at the office, an idea I reject because it will mean negotiating with his secretary who protects him from everyone, even me.

The train is crowded already. I find a seat and pretend to sleep, lulled by the rhythm of wheels on track.

*He is affection and the future, and the strength and love which
we, standing in the midst of rage and the dullness of our lives . . .*
I wish I'd brought the book with me. The words come
from Rimbaud, of course, the prose-poem '*Génie*'. Words
into Winchesters, Miss Wilcox, thank you for showing
us how. *He is love; measure perfect and reinvented . . .* But
Rimbaud is wrong, I think boldly. We're the ones crying
out for reinvention. Love is just a word, a paltry word
so overloaded with significance we no longer know what
it means. He says: love. She says: love. I say: jailbait,
chicken–shit, umbrella stand, uncle, *lâche*. You say: *finito*.
I say: OK.

The house was empty when I first got home, its windows blackened by our absence (they always are). I went
straight to the attic where I found the remnants of my
record collection and the album I sought, Léo Ferré's
Amour anarchie, which I played downstairs on Stephen's
old-fashioned stereo, always the same track, '*La mémoire
et la mer*', letting the ebb and flow of repeated sounds break
over me like the surf on Arcachon *plage*. It was cheap, it
was sentimental and I cried like hell. Then I took the record
outside and smashed it on the edge of the path, chucking
the broken pieces into the bin.

I must have looked a sight when Stephen finally came home
earlier than expected but later than hoped. With a rush of
relief I heard the turn of his key in the lock, listened while
he took off his raincoat, hung it on the peg in the hall,
put his briefcase down on the chair, first snapping the
catch to check that all his papers were there then clicking
it shut again.

*   *   *

He walks towards the kitchen then stops. Slight pause. His shoes, the ones with metal toe-caps, I hear them walking towards this room, tap-tapping on the parquet, more of a soft-shoe-shuffle as he treads on the afghan rug then a moment's silence while he stands outside the door. He feels my presence in the house despite the lack of signs. My bag lies discarded on the attic floor. Outdoor shoes kicked under the bed. Raincoat hanging safely in the gallery cloakroom that has long since closed for the night. Nothing to indicate my return but he knows I am here and I know he knows.

The door creaks open. I see his face light up when he spies me on the sofa, his not-very-handsome face that sometimes (when his clients prove exceptionally demanding) goes slack like a patient on an operating table but mostly projects the vigour of a man who looks after himself well and who – unlike his wife – sleeps easily at night. His glance strays to the mantelpiece where it lingers over two unfamiliar objects: a black-and-white illustration torn from a gallery catalogue and the dog-eared photograph of a man he doesn't know, a man with the scales of love in his eyes and a fine, impish grin.

'Stephen,' I say, trying to make my voice sound light as a heartbeat, 'there's something I must tell you. An old, old story I should have told you years ago. I thought it was a love story but it isn't, I promise you – not any more.'

That's a start, isn't it? I shall have to find the right words, of course. It won't be easy.

195

A NOTE ON THE AUTHOR

Jennifer Potter is a freelance writer, journalist and author of two previous novels, *The Taking of Agnès* and *The Long Lost Journey*. She studied French at Bristol University and now lives in North London with her son.